M000200973

Existence

Michael Piccirilli

Copyright © 2019 Michael Piccirilli
All rights reserved
First Edition

NEWMAN SPRINGS PUBLISHING
320 Broad Street
Red Bank, NJ 07701

First originally published by Newman Springs Publishing 2019

ISBN 978-1-64096-727-4 (Paperback)
ISBN 978-1-64096-728-1 (Digital)

Printed in the United States of America

I would like to dedicate this book to my daughter Sophia who is my inspiration in life and the very reason for my existence. I also would like to thank my partner in life Tania and my wonderful mother Linda for their continued support on this project.

Chapter 1

O ur world has become an apprehensive and maniacal place to exist. The American economy has begun to dissolve forcing the rest of the world to follow suit. The American dollar has lost most of its value setting the majority of the world into an economic crisis. Import and export trade has become a tale only reminisced in history classes, and governments along with its nations have focused on self-preservation at all cost. This world has become a place of survival, and only the strongest will persevere.

The United States of America has become the poster child of the economic depression and now relies on other countries for their survival. Russia has become the world's leading export for oil and now has taken its place as the world's number one super power. The United States has lost all its means of natural resources, and with its dollar being worth near nothing, they had been forced to look outside the box for securing their future. The United States has shifted its focus on offshore drilling as a means to restoring their crippled economy and rejuvenating their once proud place as head of the world's table. The United States still faces global threats from religious extremist focusing on the complete destruction of an infidel alongside powerful nations like Russia and China pushing to tap a final nail into the US coffin. The little money in their budget is used for what's left of their defense network and securing the little pride they still have. Their pride is defined as a united nation that stands tall refusing to back down from an idea that once labeled itself as indestructible.

With the United States on the brink of disaster, the nation has come together to vote in a new president, a president that represents and believes in America, a president that will lead this once proud nation's flag through these trying times. The idea of the new president begins with the offshore drilling stations in an effort to dodge the stress of raw crude being charged three times the normal value. These stations will once again allow them to regain their consistent trade of exporting and importing of oil as well as generate thousands of jobs. The flow of this valuable resource and the resurgence of market trade will strengthen their weaken economy. From the beginning, the president's campaign was the idea of offshore drilling and the restoring of the American economy. His overwhelming ambition for the success of this idea and his passion for seeing the rise of the nation he loves won him the opportunity to save his nation. As he works to make his idea a reality, the landscape of the United States is bleak; many live below the line of poverty. New York City once the most proud city in the world now is the absolute of that landscape. For years, New York was the capital of all nations, and it was symbolic of the United States but now is the definition of its nation's economic crisis. That very canvas is now painted with despair, chaos, and destruction, and very little hope shines anywhere in this once magnificent city.

It's a cold winter night on late December 2; fresh snow covers the Bronx borough of New York City. The brilliant white snow hiding the sin that has ravaged this place for several years now looks almost peaceful and without concern. As you look beyond the innocent virgin snow, the streets expose their evidence of a battered wasteland as abandoned cars rest on the empty roads, and homeless citizens with stained faces of despair search through rubbish hoping for a small morsel to eat. A small group huddles around a steel drum with an inappreciable flame hoping to keep warm as others search for kindling to help keep it burning through the night. The little heat and light reflects on their tired faces as they move closer to the growing flame. An elderly woman talks to herself as she counts cans from a local trash can but starts to cry as she realizes they hold no value. The tears are of frustration and loss of hope; life seems hardly worth living, and death seems to almost be a welcome alternative.

As the night grows colder, many people have turned in early. Sleep seems to be the best way to escape the horrible realities, with dreams of better times. Darkness has taken over the borough and is broken up by only a few working streetlights and a slightly lit window on the third floor of an apartment building above Deluca's deli. This ominous glow seems to defy the despair surrounding it along with the insomnious people inside, yet the piercing light among the chilling dark in a way pleads for the idea of hope. Inside the apartment, it is cold and dim only lit by the flicker of a TV with poor reception. In the back end of the apartment, a small glow comes from the oven as it warms the room since the landlord has no oil for the furnace. This tiny apartment is home to Vinny and Ethan, two roommates that attend a local college. They both have deep hopes of change and focus on making a difference. Vinny is studying to be a teacher and is trying for his masters in religious theory, while Ethan is majoring in ancient history and has a developed theory that the past will have the answer to today's problems and a minor in Oreo cookies. Their biggest issue even in the worst of times is their constant baseball battle between the Yankees and the Red Sox. Ethan a Boston native refuses to back down from his support for his beloved team even though he lives in enemy territory. Vinny a Bronx-born kid defiant of a few titles compared to a legacy and lifetime of titles avoids conflict, while Ethan encourages it.

"You know, if Boston spent half the money the Yankees did, we would have twenty more titles," starts Ethan. "Tonight, we beat the evil empire."

"You wish," responds Vinny. "It's business, because they always brought the crowds, the crowds brought money, and they made great business choices. They pay because they can, period."

"Overpaid whiners and that has been their tradition. We have half the payroll and championships this decade. Now that's a team," shouts back Ethan.

"Whatever," snickers Vinny as he violently taps his escape key on the computer.

"This computer sucks. I have another virus."

"You need to stay off the porn sites, ass," demands Vinny as Ethan giggles in the background. With the escape key doing nothing but making horrendous beeping noises, Vinny just pulls the plug. In complete disgust, he hops over the couch and grabs a blanket to cover his feet. With a few clicks from the remote, the TV reception gets clear, and Vinny starts to flip through the channels.

Ethan humming in the kitchen yells out, "Nice, you got it working. The game is on in twenty minutes."

"Like it matters, we win all the time," playfully responds Vinny as Ethan sits next to him with a glass of milk and a handful of Oreos. The two spat for a moment like adolescent brothers before Ethan's attention is turned to a special on ancient history and pyramids. Vinny refusing to hand over the remote flicks around a few more channels of news only to be depressed by the endless stories of murder, rape, and continual violence.

"This shit makes me sick. When will there be good stuff to watch, enough with the negative crap," barks Vinny.

"Just put on the *Discovery Channel* and the pyramids stuff," mumbles Ethan with an Oreo stuffed in his mouth.

"Aren't you tired of this stuff after reading it all day at school?" ask Vinny.

"No way, I'm telling you this isn't the first time mankind was on the brink of destruction. History repeats itself, and the answer is in the past," answers Ethan. Vinny, refusing to get into a discussion, walks to his room to find his lucky Yankee hat. Like any bachelor, his room is a mess, and he has a hard time finding the warn hat from his early childhood. The room filled with separated laundry and an unmade bed that smells of strong cologne, cheap candles, and must from cold damp walls. Finally, with some hard searching, Vinny finds his lucky warn cap that he wears with pride commending their age and history.

"Did you ever think maybe your hat is a jinx," chuckles Ethan, and with a finger from Vinny in the air, they rest on the couch to watch the game. As the game goes on, the two bicker over blown calls and each keep quoting made-up stats. The two refuse to let one gain any ground on the other as the game gets tight. There are two outs and the Yankees are up 5-3 and the bases are loaded, the Red Sox threaten in the ninth.

"They're gonna break this wide open, game over. Watch," claims Ethan; the pitch is interrupted by a news flash.

"Are you kidding me? More crap about our fucked-up planet. Put the game back on!" shouts Vinny. His adrenaline-peaked comments are held at bay as the reports seem to be worse than some mild murder or rape. This is a devastation on a large scale.

"Disasters at sea, as two oil tankers collide with the new off-shore drilling station 150 miles off the New York coastline. We now go to chopper eleven to the chaotic scene. Reports indicate that as many as two hundred people may be dead and millions of raw crude oil is pouring into the ocean. From an ecological point of view, this may be the worst disaster in history. Relief efforts are hours away at best as Russian and United States ships rush to aid the devastated area. Estimates are that over eight hundred square miles of ocean will be destroyed, and its effect may in fact severely affect the entire human population." As the images are flashed across the screen, you see nothing but twisted metal, fire, and chaos, a scene pulled from the depth of hell at best that shakes anyone watching to their very core. Vinny and Ethan sit with their mouths wide open as the news flash ends and continues with the end of the game report. As the winners of the game jump around the screen, either one seems to pay much mind. Though they sometimes argue and fight over trivial things and at times are even immature, they both know the magnitude of this event and the concern of its effect.

Vinny bringing his hands to his face asks, "What have we done?"

Ethan still eating his Oreos seems to hold back on his concern and dips his last cookie in the warming milk. He soon shows his understanding when he shows concern of the political ramification, "This is gonna get worse before it gets better. What do you think will happen when both the US and the Russians show up on the scene? Either of the two nations will want to take the blame for this disaster, and I'm sure there will be a lot of finger pointing. This will be as political as it will be environmental. Mark my words."

Ethan saying his peace starts off to the bathroom as Vinny tunes into other channels playing similar scenes. He lands on a channel that seems to have been given updated information as to the cause of the accident. The reports indicate heavy winds and rough seas were to blame, but it then reports the name of the two ships involved in the disaster, and Vinny falls back to the couch.

"It can't be," whispers Vinny, and now, this disaster may be more personal.

Chapter 2

Several blocks away, we see another brightly lit window on a fourth-floor apartment building. Just below the window rests a broken old neon sign that reads Jesus saves with hints of the once brilliant greens and reds. The damaged sign dangles over the dark alleyway dumpster casting an eerie glow over scattered rubbish. The dim light coming from the sign brings life to a painted wall filled with talented graffiti usually consumed by the morbid darkness surrounding its home in the alleyway. The accents of the melodious glow from the apartment glisten from the carefully picked pastels that color Sophia's apartment.

Sophia is a beautiful mocha-skinned young woman in her early twenties. She sits in an oversized couch filled with large pillows in a pure cotton oversized tee shirt preparing for the next day's events. Sophia seems to be very soft-spoken, maybe even shy, but nothing could be farther from the truth. She is filled with animosity toward today's society, the society that has destroyed the earth, economy, and future's way of life. She believes in God and women's rights; she believes in holding all people accountable and plans on letting them all know it. As an avid protester, she finalizes the poster for tomorrow's big rally on animal cruelty. With attentions turned to the poster and her tofu salad, she barely hears the special report on the recent chaotic events. In the background, she hears her cell phone ring, and she quickly hops off the couch to answer. When she answers it, she hears a friend franticly muttering words and barely understands anything she is saying. As she pours hot water to make her favorite herbal green tea, her friend finally becomes clear and asks.

"Aren't you watching the news?"

Feeling caught off guard, Sophia sips some tea as she turns up the volume to the TV. As the report continues and Sophia begins to comprehend the report, her eyes begin to fill with tears. The report soon flashes images live from the devastated area, and Sophia drops the phone and tea and covers her face hoping that when she looks again, it was all a dream. She slowly peers through her opening fingers and sees it is in fact real and drops to the couch and cries. As the images continue, she can't help but think of the effects this will have on the animals and the environment. Her emotions uncontrollably run wild with anger and sadness, quickly consuming her entire being. She hears her name being called and remembers her friend on the phone. She picks it up, and with as much composure as she can muster, she asks.

"What are we going to do, Julie?"

"We make our voices heard. We rally at the docks at dawn and remind them that this will not be tolerated!" shouts her friend.

"Meet me here at five thirty and bring the girls tomorrow. We will be one voice, and we will be heard!" blasts Sophia. And the two hang up and prepare for tomorrow's protest. This is Sophia and what she lives for; even the people who refuse to listen will hear her.

Chapter 3

Back in Washington, the president sits with his top advisors and prepares for tomorrow's speech about the tides of the economy and the rise of a once powerful nation. President Anderson is the very definition of America, defined by the struggle and pride of a great nation. Raised in Peekskill, New York, he came from a broken home and was introduced to a life of crime and gangs at an early age. Though out of sight of New York City, Peekskill rests only forty-five minutes from the city and has many of its influences. At an early age, Terence Anderson was different; though he was surrounded by adversity, he seemed wise beyond his years. He avoided things he felt were morally wrong, and when he turned eighteen, he joined the US Navy. Taking the lessons he learned as a young black male in New York and focusing that energy on his new career, he moved up in rank quickly. After three years, he was accepted into BUD/S training program and graduated as the top navy seal of his class. For several years, he would dedicate his life to his country and was prepared to die for it at any time. The years he gave to his country and the life he lived before the military, as well as after, created the man that will take this country out of the hole it is in. His mother supported him till she died from breast cancer while he was on tour in the Middle East. His mother's death was the hardest thing to overcome and found tremendous support in his best friend Daniel Gray. Daniel was an orphan as a child and grew up in Chicago. He had many things in common with President Anderson as a member of his seal team opening the door for a strong lasting friendship. For years, they fought side by side in the Navy, and today, he is his most trusted advisor and the admiral of the Atlantic Fleet.

The president has kept his word during his campaign and has generated a 40 percent increase to the American economy. The offshore drilling station has created thousands of jobs and revenue and is beginning to restore the United States as a global pillar to a shaky foundation. The room seems positive as they discuss the focus on the president's speech.

One advisor proudly stands up and tells the room, "I am proud to say that we have returned 100 percent of the money borrowed from social security, and we are currently six months ahead of schedule on all budget guidelines we have for the fiscal year." With the room filled with cheers, the president stands up.

"I have never been as proud as I am today of the people in this room. Tomorrow I will smile for the first time in a long time and hold my head up high as I address our great nation," states the president. They seem to be content and begin to close their books when a navy lieutenant interrupts their final remarks. The officer lowers his head to get closer as he whispers in the president's ear and points to a laptop facing him. The officer steps back as the president sits back in his chair.

"What have we done?" whispers the president.

The room grows silent as they wait to see what has caused him concern. With a crackle in his voice and a tear in his eye, the president rises up and stands before the group he just moments ago praised so proudly.

"Within the last hour, a disaster occurred that may very well cripple this nation. Moments ago, I stood before you proud, but now, I feel defeated, and I may very well have failed you all. Two freighters carrying millions of gallons of raw crude oil under heavy seas collided with each other and then destroyed our offshore drilling station. The devastation is biblical. Many have died, and the effects will destroy us economically, environmentally, and perhaps even spiritually. We must now address a battered nation and help them through what may be a fatal blow. This my friends will be our biggest challenge yet, but if nothing else we must stand by this great nation."

The crowd with lowered heads begins to make preparations for the press release and prepare for what will be a long night. Hours and hours go by as the data and hellish scene dominates the room. The president knows no matter how hard they try, anything written will be manufactured and impersonal. He knows that the pages in front of him now will what define his legacy and prepare to face his fate. The president maintaining his posture looks at the well-written speech he planned on delivering moments from now. He scans a few lines and grins at the irony. Losing control, he crumbles up the speech into a ball and throws it against the wall as if he could throw it through it. Feeling guilty about his action, he sits back in the soft leather chair and prays asking for strength and forgiveness. He stands up and puts on his tailored suit jacket, takes a big breath, and heads down the hall. The hall seems endless as each step seems to hurt his soul, and the echo of his shoes is almost deafening. He reaches the pressroom, takes another deep breath, and says, "Let's get this over with."

The media gathers all eagerly anticipating the president's response to the tragedy. In a small room filled with unfamiliar faces, the president addresses a now shaken nation. He reads from the cue cards and soon is blinded by emotion from the carefully written announcement. He feels at this point that it's necessary to talk to the nation not as the president but as an American. Going against his advisor's recommendations, he politely asks the cue cards to be lowered. With a brief pause, he starts to speak from his heart; he begins talk to the Americans as a friend and asks that as a nation they unite and help recover from this devastating event.

"My friends, no cue card will ever express my feelings today. I want to talk to you from my heart and not from some well-scripted politically correct speech. We have several ships rushing to the scene in hopes of saving any lives that may be in jeopardy. There will be several coast guard ships docked in New York harbor bringing qualified volunteers to the scene due to the short supply of enlisted soldiers available. I ask that anyone wanting to help to donate blood, nonperishable foods and supplies to the New York Bay and to do so in an organized manner. The success of this recovery will be based on the strength of the American people. This will be our most challenging battle, and in return, it can also become our finest hour. I ask you to be the Americans that are the foundation to this country, the same Americans that defined freedom led by our forefathers, the Americans that pulled together after 9/11, and to be the same Americans today that remain united. Stand strong, unified, and I promise we will win the day."

With no comment from the media other than loud silence, the president walks away and thanks them for their understanding. The room's silence has grown uncomfortable as crews clean up their cameras and belongings. In the back of the room next to an American flag rests a crucifix and old gift from the Vatican in the fifties. With the room now cleared, a *Time* magazine reporter sees a young boy maybe five years old kneeling and praying at the crucifix in a traditional stance with clasped hand tight to his chest. The image would become an American symbol of faith in their country and will inspire a torn nation fueled by hope.

Chapter 4

The news has been flashing images all night, and Vinny and Ethan are drained. Ethan is concerned about Vinny because the last report seemed to jolt him into a panic mode, and he has begun to rip apart the house.

"What are you doing, Vinny?" asks Ethan.

"I'm looking for the postcard my brother sent me before his last deployment," responds Vinny.

"Dude, it's still on the fridge, next to the calendar." points Ethan.

The postcard is the last time Vinny has heard from his big brother, and the separation has been hard on him. Rushing to the refrigerator, Vinny grabs the postcard and begins to look it over. On the postcard was a picture of a snow-filled scene in Alaska. Vinny flips over the image and begins to reread the brief letter from his brother who was deployed three months ago on large boat for transport. When the offshore drilling station was complete, it opened up thousands of jobs ranging from working on the drilling station to all means of export. Vinny's brother Louis was quick to land a job as a deckhand on a new oil freighter since he was a merchant marine and also as a coast guard veteran. The letter only discussed his job and where he was ported, but that's all Vinny was looking for.

"Found it, the Megedon. That's it, goddamn it," shouts Vinny as he rushes to look for a phone.

"What the hell is a Megedon?" asks Ethan as he chases Vinny around the apartment.

"It's the ship my brother was on!" shouts Vinny. "Where's the friggin' phone?"

"Under the blanket on the couch. Why does the ship your brother was on matter?" questions Ethan.

"Not was, is, and if you would stop eating those Oreos, you would hear that it's the same ship that is involved in the incident out on the Atlantic!" shouts Vinny.

Ethan's heart drops and rushes over to grab the phone and tosses it to Vinny. Vinny begins to dial out to his father in Pelham but hears nothing but a busy signal followed by a message that all lines are busy, trying over and over to get through with no luck forcing him to become frantic. He begins to flash through channel after channel hoping for some breaking news and is soon interrupted by the president's address to the nation. Vinny is shaking; he is riddled with anxiety and tries to take in the words from the president that he has a deep admiration for. After listening to the heartfelt delivery by the president, Vinny feels compelled to do more than just sit and wait. Vinny tries one more time to call his family and draws impatient as he again gets the same message. With his patience now wearing thin, he begins to gather his shoes and winter hat while headed to the front door where he grabs for his winter jacket.

"Where the hell you think you're going?" ask Ethan with a defensive tone, then Vinny shouts back.

"Dead or alive my brother will need me. I'm sure they will bring the bodies and survivors to the bay. I'm going to be there to help find him or identify him!" Then he lowers his head and says in an apologetic tone, "I can't just sit here and do nothing."

With all their adolescent-type bickering and endless debates, Ethan knows that his friend needs him, and those trivial things mean nothing to him compared to their friendship. Ethan loves him like a brother and feels it's necessary to bring some reality into the picture.

"It's almost midnight, and the first rescue vessel hasn't even arrived on the scene. It will be hours of search time and hours back to the bay. Let's get some sleep, and I will make a call. I have a friend that works on a pier down there, and maybe I can get us through the fences," suggests Ethan as he comforts Vinny who has now begun to break down on the couch. Vinny is proud and hides his face by turning away to hide a tear trickling down his cheek and with a break in his voice says, "You're right. I'm just going to get a few hours of sleep, and I will be up and out by five."

"You mean we, right? There is no way I'm gonna let you do this on your own. I'll be up too, and we will find him together," says Ethan as he extends his hand out to his friend.

"I love you, man. I mean it. I couldn't do it without you," responds Vinny as the two go to their rooms. Vinny already dressed for tomorrow wraps himself up with several blankets soaked in the cologne drenched edges. He can't help but feel useless and battles the anxiety for almost an hour before the stress exhausts him, and he falls asleep.

Chapter 5

I n the silence of the freezing ocean floats a magnificent vessel called the Lexington II, and it looks almost mystical surrounded by the dense sea smoke embracing it. The lower decks smell of ocean air with a cool breeze making for a comfortable night's sleep. In the most forward section of the quarterdeck sleeps Admiral Gray. His room is decorated with awards and several dress uniforms freshly pressed for the morning's award ceremony. The admiral in a deep sleep becomes restless as he hears tapping come from the outside of his door.

"Admiral, Sir, you are requested on the bridge. I was told to tell you it's a class five emergency."

"Thank you, ensign. I will be top side in a moment," says the admiral with a sleepy tone.

The admiral looks around the room and sees only dress uniforms available and slips on his crisp dress whites. He stretches trying to force his exhaustion away from his public character that is meant for the press several hours from now. His quarters though better than standard are tight but organized and have a smell of fresh shoe polish and spray starch. He is old school and still prides himself on the mirror shine. He puts on his dress shoes and the crisp lines on his dress uniform. He walks out the hatch and begins to rush through the ship as he finishes the final touches on the meticulous uniform and enters the bridge where he is met by the captain.

"Admiral on deck," shouts a sailor as everyone rises to their feet.

"At ease, gentleman," says the admiral as he reads through the class five emergencies. He quickly says his orders and puts the ship on high alert. Being that, he is the highest-ranking officer on the ships he assumes command. He looks around the bridge and makes aware his officers of the issue at hand.

"Gentleman, it appears that a disaster has occurred thirty miles east of here. It appears that two vessels have collided with the off-shore drilling station, and we are now in charge of recovery and assessment," notifies the admiral.

An ensign alarmed by the order addresses the obvious, "Admiral, we are a skeleton crew set up for PR, and the lower decks are filled with media. We aren't prepared for this mission."

"We are the closest to the scene and may be the only hope for any of the survivors. The media will just have to help. Besides, this is a hell of a story they should be thanking us. Call ahead to Boston and Norfolk. We will need assistance from the Atlantic fleet. Now wake the ship, and let's make way. Time is of the essence!" orders the admiral.

The Lexington II was on hand in the New York Harbor for an award ceremony, and they took a two-day trial run for the media. The ship is one of the newest ships to harness stealth technologies and can produce more than seventy knots on calm waters. The admiral was on hand to award several members of the crew with medals for the trials on the new ship. The media was on hand to report on the ship and get a tour of the navy's newest crown jewel. With all other options too far away, the president called upon his friend to once again help his country.

With the order for full speed ahead, the Lexington II and its limited crew make way in the Atlantic and toward the hellish scene. The ship soon becomes alive as the crew and media scurry around the deck and passageways. The admiral sits in the command chair reading over the reports coming from Washington. His concerns fall on the safety of his crew and civilians on board as the reports become more detailed. His biggest concern is the rescue of any survivors but can't help but feel apprehensive as he realizes that the second ship was Russian.

"Captain, tell the gunnies to ready all weapons as a precaution. I never was one for surprises," asks the admiral.

Captain Gamble alerts all gunners' mates and their crews to make ready the ship's weapon systems, and soon, the crew buzzes with rumors of a possible battle. With the ships racing toward the scene, the admiral gets on the loud speaker and addresses his crew and media.

"All hands, there has been an accident in the Atlantic, and we are on a recovery mission. The president has asked me directly to assess the damage and save as many people as we can. I also feel compelled to alert you that there will be Russians in the area, and it is the reason for me being cautious. I must remind you of the rules of engagement and that there will be no fire from a US ship unless provoked and only on my order."

As the crew continues to ready, the ship media personnel begin to show signs of concern asking to speak with the admiral. Captain Gamble understanding their concerns assures them that they will be safe and will have front-row seats for the story of the century. With the revelation of the magnitude of the story, the media becomes blinded and seems to disregard their concerns of well-being and heads to the weather deck with hopes of getting first glances and photo of the carnage. The admiral watches as his crew works to ready his ship and shakes his head as the media offers no help in preparation.

"I could never do that. Live on other people's misery. They are all waiting for the big story that will get that big paycheck. It's a sad world we live in. God help us all," remarks the admiral as they close in on the devastated scene.

Chapter 6

The daylight has barely broke the darkness of night, and Vinny is up gathering all he needs to head to the pier. Ethan who never was a morning person drags himself into the living room trying to wipe the sleep from his eyes.

"Did you even sleep?" asks Ethan

"Hardly. Every time I closed my eyes that damn scene flashed in my head and my brother's face," replies Vinny.

As Ethan tries to wake up, Vinny hands him a fresh cup of coffee and an English muffin. He has taken the liberty to load up Ethan's backpack and gathered some warm clothes for the day ahead.

"Light and sweet right?" asks Vinny as he eagerly presses Ethan to get ready.

"Relax, buddy. My friend is expecting us at six thirty. We will get behind the fences, and we will find your brother," says Ethan in a sympathetic tone.

The coffee has begun to kick in, and Ethan stands at the door bundled up and ready to go. With the morning light shining on the city, the two determined friends embark on their journey to the city pier.

Several miles away, a highly caffeinated Sophia rushes around her apartment trying to get organized for the morning rally. She brushes her hair back into a tight ponytail and finishes the last of her wholegrain muffin. Sophia looks at her watch and realizes she has a few moments to catch her breath. She turns on the TV and watches the morning news to see if anything has happened in regard to the accident. Only moments after the weather, it's reported that our navy ships are arriving on the scene and have started to access the seriousness of the accident and have begun their search and rescue attempts. In disgust, she throws her hands up at the TV and shouts.

"To hell with the assholes that caused this mess. Fix the problem and stop the contamination from spreading!"

With only moments before she has a full screaming match with her TV, she is interrupted by the buzzer from her friends in the downstairs lobby. She grabs her well-made signs and jacket and rushes down the stairs to meet her rally partners. At first glance, their gear and the overall turnout inspire her. They have been waiting for this for a long time and have gone almost overboard with their symbols of protest. Most of them will be throwing up their hand-painted signs of cartoonish pictures and protesting slogans. One friend seemed compelled to cover a stuffed animal in black paint, while another is dressed in a cardboard-made oil drum and nothing else.

"You're going to freeze at the rally," giggles Sophia, asking him to put some clothes on.

Encouraged, the group now heads out together to fight the demons of society and make their voices heard.

With only a few blocks left before they reach the pier, Vinny and Ethan begin to see signs of the rescue efforts underway. The air is cold and heavy as overhead. They see several helicopters in a tight formation headed east toward the bay. In front, a strong military presence is evident as soldiers and camouflaged trucks begin to line the streets waking the normally mundane streets. A horn startles them as a troop transporter tries to squeeze by them full of volunteers.

"We need to go to the west gate, and if anyone asks, we are members of the union volunteering for metal salvaging, okay?" whispers Ethan.

With a slight nod, Vinny acknowledges their story, and the two push forward finding the best route to get to the west gate among the maze of government vehicles. In the distance, a large green sign with white letters reads out "Gate 7," and the two rushes forward hoping to find Ethan's friend. The entire area is surrounded by every possible organization, both military and civilian. On the outside of the gate are several volunteers donating blood, while others are giving them coffee, donuts, bottled water, and hot cocoa. Vinny gets a little emotional as he takes in the scene of unity and compassion, an image that seems to be almost a forgotten presence. Though many people may have died, he sees all these people here for his brother and feels touched. Ethan less attached to the situation sees the scene as a disappointment rather than encouraging.

"I remember 9/11 when New York came together after the attacks. Then I remember them slowly forgetting that day and becoming the same people they were before, filled with anger and resentment. I wonder if this will be any different?" says Ethan.

Vinny, almost offended, glares back at Ethan as if it was a personal dig and continues to make his way toward the gate entrance. Vinny quickly loses sight of his frustration toward Ethan's comment as it's dwarfed by the anger-filled comments coming from a rowdy group of protesters at the gate's entrance. With his focus heavy on the protesters, Vinny walks within feet of the loud crowd with signs waving around in his face.

Sophia filled with anger seems fueled by the amount of people there to volunteer to help with the search and rescue and the lack of support to protest the responsibility of holding someone accountable. With an overwhelming amount of disgust, she shouts out at the volunteers and their purpose for being there. Throughout her life, she was always defined as a bitch, but the fact is she likes people; she just doesn't understand why they need to destroy things to move forward. With a world full of problems on her shoulders, she becomes louder and louder and continues as she is encouraged by her friends. With her adrenaline pumping, she grabs the microphone and shouts, losing sight of some words amplified from her mouth, and gets carried away.

"Is this the America we want?" shouts Sophia

"Do we need to destroy life to preserve it?"

"You expect me to mourn the people who died destroying our planet? Hell no!"

"They deserved to die, and I hope they suffer for it in hell!"

Before anything else can be said, a light tap on her shoulder interrupts her. She stands face-to-face with a young man who asks her in a calm voice.

"Can I ask you something?"

Sophia looking bewildered and annoyed by the young man but gives him a moment to speak. He unzips his jacket and from his inside pocket pulls out several pictures and starts to go through them one by one. The pictures are of him and another man slightly taller in what would seem to be better times.

"This was last year at the Yankee game we caught a home run ball. This was his surprise birthday party. He hates surprises, and this one is his going away barbeque. He got drunk. That's why his face looks like that." He says with a slight grin.

"Why does that matter to me? Why show me these pictures?" asks Sophia.

"So if you see his body you would know a little about a great man and how much he is loved and that no one deserves to be out there to die alone, here."

The young man hands over a picture of himself and the other man, "Keep it. I have a lifetime full of them right here," says the young man as he taps his head.

Sophia completely caught off guard realizes she may have been too rash and feels embarrassed by the comments shouted only moments ago. As the young man walks away, she shouts out to him, "I'm sorry. I let my emotions get the best of me."

With the man waiving it off, Sophia watches as he meets up with another man waiting at the gate. Eager to make it up to him, she runs away from her friends and grabs him by the shoulder.

"Hey, let me make it up to you. I will help you find him!" claims Sophia.

"I'm all set," replies the young man.

Being the determined-minded woman she is, the persistent Sophia won't back down and insists on introducing herself. The young man, realizing that he has no choice, acknowledges her and turns around to listen.

"My name is Sophia Cruz. You are?"

With her hand stretched out, they shake hands, but they are pulled aside by the young man's friend before he could reply.

"Okay. We are good. Let's get inside. There's a volunteer boat going to the scene right now. If we hurry up, we can get on board and be one of the first civilian boats there," says his friend.

With time running short, the young man thanks Sophia for her support and begins to walk away. Sophia feeling obligated to help this young man follows him beyond the gate. At the far left dock sits a 110-ft boat with the engines beginning to rumble and the crew undoing the lines. The young man and his friend rush to get on board but soon notice they have Sophia in tow.

"What are you doing?" asks the young man.

"I said I was going to help you find your friend," responds Sophia.

The young man realizes he has no time to argue and agrees and helps her on board. As the vessel pulls away from the dock, Sophia once again presses to introduce herself.

"I never did get your name. I'm Sophia."

With a pause, the young man looks over his shoulder and addresses her request.

"I'm Vinny, this is my friend Ethan, and we are here to find my brother."

With the vessel moving out to the Atlantic, they are greeted with winter ocean air and rough seas, but nothing will keep them from reaching their goal.

Chapter 7

The glow of the horizon becomes brilliant as the sun introduces a new day. Taking in the calm of the morning, the admiral sips from his routine coffee and prepares for the mission ahead. The admiral has always admired the ocean's mornings; it always reveals the magnificence of the world and humbles even the most inflated ego. As the sun reveals more of the Atlantic, it soon becomes evident the amount of destruction caused from the tragic accident. Staring at the water, Admiral Gray watches as the beautiful ocean he loved for years turns black and hints of rainbow pastels reflect off the leaking oil. The oil has already spread over a one-mile radius and has got so thick that the wake from the ship rolls off the bow with no break or white caps. The only sign of the ocean is the sun reflecting off the scales of dead fish unable to escape the grasp of the contaminating oil. Soon, a fiery glow reveals the twisted metal of the deep-sea drilling station, and the scene hypnotizes the admiral. The ships have split apart but refuse to find a watery grave as they cling to the twisted base of the drilling station. The fire leaks from one ship to another on bridges of leaked oil, and it's clear it made its way to the station that had an immense explosion. Parts of the station are leaned over into the ocean exposing its core which is projecting oil and fire hundreds of feet into the air coating everything in its reach. In all his years on the sea, he has never seen this much devastation or man-made evil. The admiral calls to the bridge for a full stop as bodies begin to liter the ocean's surface.

"Keep them away from the props," shouts the admiral.

"Yes, sir," answers a deckhand fresh from boot camp.

The admiral sets off the alarm, and his crew begins to lower smaller boats into the darkened ocean to search for survivors and collect the ones who weren't so lucky. This is a lot to ask for crew-members that thought this was a PR trip as some become notice-ably sick as they bring them up to the Lexington's deck. The bodies rest on the deck covered in blood and oil as the ocean continues to burn making some so scorched they can't be identified. The admiral walks around the deck frustrated by the harsh images and fact they haven't seen any survivors. As one of the medics begins to zip up a body bag, the admiral sees the chard hand accented by the shine of a wedding band.

"Petty officer, let me see his face," asks Admiral Gray.

"Admiral, he has no face or left leg or two-thirds of his torso. Even with all this oil, sharks are ripping them apart," replies the petty officer.

Before the admiral can even respond, the flash of a reporter who wanted a close up of the mutilated body and wedding band blinds him.

"Don't you have any fucking respect? Back up before you go in the bag with him," shouts the admiral.

"Come on, this story is huge, an opportunity of a lifetime," responds the reporter.

"All press below decks, now!" orders the admiral.

As some deckhands round up the scattered media, the admiral's attention is turned once again to the waters as he hears a soft cry for help. The admiral rushes around the deck trying to find where the cries are coming from. Still dressed in his ceremonial whites, he begins to lean over the rails hoping to see a sign of a survivor disre-garding the stains that the rails are putting on the virgin whites. In the distance, a crewmember calls out to the admiral.

"Over there, admiral."

The admiral looks at a twisted ball of metal that has encaged two young children while the ocean grasps at them like a predator to prey. The young boy clinches on to a younger little girl as they hold on for their dear life. The admiral notices the ignited oil creeping closer to them, as the young boy seems to be losing grip of the tired girl.

"My god, he must have been holding on to her all night," shouts the admiral. A crewmember calls over to the admiral but before he finishes his sentence, the admiral leaps into treacherous waters with no concern for himself. The admiral covered in oil swims, dodging debris and burning ocean to save the children from a horrific death. Every inch feels like a mile as the vicious heat seems to char the admiral's face that is quickly extinguished by the winter Atlantic. With only a few feet till he reaches them, a large explosion engulfs the area in fire spreading black smoke and ignited debris around him. The admiral avoiding the chaos dives below the surface and continues toward the horrified children. From under the water above him, he sees the feet of the children and darts toward the surface of twisted metal and fire. As soon as he breaks the surface, he is met with screams of the frightened children and the evil heat from the surrounding flames. He quickly grabs the two children and tells them to hold their breath. As the children grasp for air, the admiral plunges below to free them of the twisted metal and determined fire. As they swim free and reach the surface, an ocean of relentless flames circling from every direction greets them. With no time to rest, the admiral swims with all his vigor pushing metal and fire out of his way and shielding the children from harm. The surface temperature from the flames has become so hot the admiral's face feels burnt only distracted by the sting of the salt water. He grabs the little girl with his right arm and tells the boy to wrap his arms around the admiral's neck. Pain settles in as the admiral's left arm drenched in oil begins to catch fire. Doing all he can to smother the flames, his focus is the children as he continues to swim toward his ship and crew that has lowered a recovery basket. As he gets close, he hears the rumble of the massive motor and props that muffles as he tires and his head is hard to keep above water. The water breaks against the hull making it difficult to get near the rescue basket; the admiral continues to get smacked up against the ship trying to keep the children safe forcing the charred oil and tainted salt water to fill his mouth. The admiral begins to feel fatigued and in a last minute effort heaves the children into the rescue basket exerting all the energy he has left. The black water rushes over his face and the drag from the ship seems to suck him deep in the heartless abyss. With the crew screaming to the admiral to grab a line, he finds it impossible to muster any strength to hold his weight and to pull himself from the chaos. As the fire-covered water rushes overhead and a mass of frigid water fills his final breath tasting of fresh diesel, the admiral watches as the children are pulled to safety.

Back in Washington, President Anderson looks over pages of data with his advisors. Hoping a resolve will leap off the pages, the president begins to lose patience. President Anderson, a bit overwhelmed, steps back from the mounds of data and tries to gather his thoughts when an advisor's assistant rushes into the room holding a phone. President Anderson, who is in no mood for conversation, waves off the assistant.

"Not now. This isn't the time."

"Sir, I think it's important. It's the captain in the Atlantic," responds the assistant.

"The captain, where's the admiral?"

He has a bad feeling in the pit of his stomach as he picks up the phone. The captain starts briefing him of the scene and that there hasn't been signs of many survivors in the freezing waters littered with fire and oil hinting that there were perhaps some. The captain's tone mellows, and his voice breaks as he then alerts him to the brave heroics of his friend the admiral.

"Without any hesitation, he leaped into the water and rushed to their aid, sir."

"And where's the admiral now?"

"Sir, his efforts where exhausting, and he was lost in the churned water and fire. His only concerns were those kids," says the captain with a broken tone

"I don't care. Alive or dead, he comes home. Understand, Captain?"

"Yes, sir Mr. President."

President Anderson's eyes begin to fill with water as he realizes the fate of his friend seems grim. His mind races with reflections of their past twenty plus years and the thousands of memories they shared. He remembers their family vacations and fun-filled barbeques along with their danger-filled missions and the admiral's passion for protecting his team. The president stares down on his exposed forearm from a rolled-up tailored dress shirt. He looks at a faded trident tattoo and feels empty and lost as a large piece of him appears to have vanished into the Atlantic. As the phone still pressed up against his ear, he hears some commotion in the background.

"Bring him up on the deck and get the medic here now," shouts the captain.

The president, eager to know what is going on, yells into the phone trying to get the captain's attention. With no response on the other end, the president paces along the length of mahogany table silencing the people in the room. He squeezes the phone and presses his ear hoping to hear anything of the turbulent noise turning his ear red. In an effort to get someone's attention, he yells into the phone and is soon answered by a familiar voice.

"I'm okay, Terence, just a little older than I thought," says the admiral.

"You fucking nut, when you get home, I'm going to kick your ass," shouts back the president.

While the two argue about the actions of the aging admiral, the captain interrupts to point out a problem in the horizon. The admiral cuts off the president still trying to argue his point.

"Terence, we have an issue."

Paused by the comment, President Anderson asks what the issue is and is told that a Russian fleet has shown up to evaluate the accident. They have shown up in force with two submarines and several war ships including a new state-of-the-art aircraft carrier. The concern of the admiral is that they are in battle formations, and if they attack, he is vulnerable. The rest of the Atlantic fleet is making way to the scene but is about an hour away; they are sitting ducks.

The president reminds the admiral of their rules of engagement and alerts them of the fact that several civilian ships should be arriving soon to assist in the search and rescue. "At all cost, protect your men and the lives on your ship. Caution the civilian's boats that show up. The last thing we want is an incident that will cost further lives!" demands the president.

The admiral continues to describe the film that is engulfing the disaster scene but is at a loss for words as it gets stranger. His attention is then brought to the bow as the hellish portrait that has now changed and has begun to scare the crew. Though the Russian poses a threat, it's not the pressing concern for the admiral who focuses on a new circumstance. With some hesitation, the admiral contacts President Anderson about the landscape change.

"Terence, I don't know how to explain this. It appears the fires are dying out, and a weird film seems to be coming through the oil spill throughout the entire radius of the accident."

"Is it Russian?" asks the president.

"I don't think so. They seem to be as confused as we are."

The admiral continues to describe the film that seems to be taking over the disaster scene in detail but has at a loss for words as stranger it gets. With each word, the president thinks the admiral is pulling a joke on the sometimes-gullible president. Soon realizing that this is not a joke, the scene turns from concerning to weird.

"Okay, all the debris is being pulled into the center. The oil, metal, and even the bodies are condensing like someone is cleaning up our mess," explains the admiral.

Over the next several minutes, the entire accident has been contained to a compressed two-hundred-yard radius. Around the ship, there seems to be no sign of any oil, bodies, or any debris. In the distance, you hear an eerie noise of all the twisted metal being pulled together forcing the debris field to get smaller and smaller.

A crewmember notifies the bridge that the remainder of the Atlantic fleet will arrive ahead of schedule on the port side, while several civilian boats have arrived on starboard. The admiral has comfort in the fact that he now has the Atlantic fleet at his back but now has concern that there are civilians on the scene. The admiral alerts the fleet and orders the crew to alert status and begins to hail the civilian ships when the already-confusing spectacle changes yet again.

Chapter 8

The rough sea has begun to make Sophia nauseous, and Ethan watches her as she leans over the iced-up side rails. The boat is filled with volunteer firefighters and EMTs all anxious to help in the recovery, but no one has a pill for seasickness. Ethan offers Sophia an Oreo cookie, and the smell instantly forces her to throw up all over the side. Vinny slightly amused hands her a toilette to wipe her face that still has a green tone. In the distance, they see the ghostly silhouettes of several navy ships against the morning sun and know they are only moments away from their destination. Vinny becoming anxious begins to look around the boat hoping to get a glimpse of debris or signs of his brother. Feeling a little better, Sophia remains compelled to help him look, so she rushes to the opposite side to look for any signs of survivors. As their boat comes along the starboard side of the navy ships, the volunteers are caught off guard by the site of the tight circle in which the debris has been gathered. Vinny is amazed at the fact that there is no oil anywhere, and Sophia is thrilled with the fact that it seems the animals will be safe. The lead navy ship, standing proud among an older fleet, orders all civilian ships to stand back with the evidence of a Russian military presence. Vinny becomes very concerned about his brother as he watches all the debris mashed together in a mysterious circle along with the threat of the Russian war ships. Ethan who displays his cable-induced knowledge of the Russian fleet also expresses some concern.

"I saw those ships on *Discovery Channel*. That is the Frunze of the Kirov class, a badass battle cruiser. That huge aircraft carrier is the Varyag, and those are three battleships are from the Sovremenny class. The Varyag is rumored to have the most advanced fighters on board, the Su-57."

"You know all that from TV?" asks Sophia.

"Yeah, and the Internet. I get bored a lot," responds Ethan.

"Try living with him," jokes Vinny.

With the joking aside, their attention is drawn to the constricting circle of debris that has now begun to encase the entire accident in a sheer bubble, gathering it together like a correlated package.

"What the hell you make of that, Vinny?" asks Ethan.

"How the hell do I know? You're the discovery buff! Wasn't that on cable?" answers Vinny.

"It's mother nature fighting back!" shouts Sophia.

As the three debate the image, in front of them they hear distance alarms ringing from both the US fleet and the Russian's. The captain of the volunteer ship orders everyone below decks for safety, but Vinny won't budge. Vinny continues to defy the orders given with his search over the rails but is soon yelled at by the captain.

"Get below decks now before things get crazy out here. Those alarms are for battle stations," alerts the captain.

"I just wanna look for my brother," replies Vinny.

"You won't find shit if you're dead, young man," taunts the captain.

The expressed opinions of the captain make sense, and Vinny heads below decks till it is safe to continue his search. When Vinny gets below, he sees the group of volunteers huddled together nervous of the outcome and second guessing their decision to assist in the recovery. Vinny, looking around the group of scared faces, tries to find Ethan and Sophia. In the back corner, standing together, Vinny sees them waving their arms trying to catch his attention. Vinny takes several steps to meet them but is alarmed by some loud whistles he hears topside echoed by a hum below his feet. He leaps in Ethan's direction and questions the noises that have begun to get louder.

"What the hell are those noises?" asks Vinny.

Before Ethan can answer the question, a loud bang rattles the boat causing the volunteers to yell out in fear. Sophia gets close to Vinny as a loud whistle seems to be getting progressively closer. Vinny out of instinct embraces Sophia and reaches over to Ethan trying to keep his friends close. Only inches away from grabbing Ethan, the whistle becomes deafening, and Vinny is hurled away from Sophia and Ethan as he is immersed by a brilliant heated burst; then everything goes black.

Chapter 9

As the opaque bubble continues to consume the ravaged landscape, the admiral waits on a distant enemy. Continuing to be over prepared, the admiral calls to the other ships to inventory their ordinance. With each moment, the air thickens with tension as it becomes evident that neither party is comfortable with the other. With the uncomfortable silence looming, the admiral makes another call to President Anderson to advise him of the vesicle and the Russians on the opposite side of it. Knowing he is outgunned, he asks the president for some welcome advice.

"Terence, I'm out of my league. I don't know if this thing is natural or man-made, but I know it's not us. The Russians are on high alert and have taken on battle formations. I just don't know if it is directed at us or this thing!"

"Stand down, Admiral. It is our goal to have a peaceful presence, and I need to explain we are on a search and rescue mission," expresses the president.

"I understand, Terence, but I do not want to sit and wait to be attacked. I'm going to hail the flagship and express our peaceful intentions," answers the admiral.

"Kitten gloves, Daniel. They are begging for a reason okay?" says the president.

"You know me," giggles the admiral and disconnects from the White House frequency. With some concern of the admiral's history, the president alerts some advisors to prepare for a possible attack in the Atlantic.

As the admiral prepares to hail the Russian fleet, his lieutenant shouts, "We are under fire, sir!"

Large eruptions of random rounds splash several yards ahead of the admiral's ship. The admiral quickly calls for battle stations but realizes that the aimless rounds are in fact targeting the milky vesicle. The substance seems to reflect the rounds and redirects them toward the US fleet. With no regard to the US fleet, rounds begin to whistle by the admiral's ship misting water on deck from near misses. Unwilling to compromise the safety of his fleet, the admiral orders to return fire but is interrupted by a petty officer on deck.

"Admiral, you need to see this. The ocean is glowing in translucent colors as far as I can see. They are getting brighter by the minute, and some of the men say they see objects moving below the surface as incredible speeds."

The admiral draws his attention to the port side of the ship and watches as the tone of the ocean turns from the blue that he has lived for to brilliant shades of pink, teal, and purple. He then realizes that the Russians have stopped firing, and they are as concerned as he is about what lies beneath. The admiral allows his curiosity to disregard his safety as he leans of the small rail to get a better view of the objects below the surface. The admiral who understands national security makes sure that the media is secure below and that all hands are safe and continues to watch as the ocean glows brighter from the mysterious objects below. As he watches the flashes of light, he begins to see forms and shapes whipping by at incredible speeds. He realizes this can't be Russian or even man-made but knows it's definitely manufactured. Airing on the side of caution, he orders his crew on alert, and the alarms once again sound. The admiral realizes he will be needed on the bridge; he turns to head topside when small splashes of water catches his attention. Once again allowing curiosity to get the better of him, he turns and watches as thousands of orbs break the ocean surface. They shine of chrome and are about eight feet in diameter with a ring that extends around their center mass. They are silent and float motionless about five feet from the surface in a grid-like pattern. One very close to the hull of the ship appears to have a vibrating ripple throughout the entire mystical sphere. The admiral watches as a light hum overwhelms the silence of his crew and the active ocean.

Once again, the admiral turns to head to the bridge when a deckhand yells out, "Look at that!"

Medium-sized craft emerge from below the surface and pair up next to each of the mysterious spheres. These craft are shaped like a spade on a deck of cards but have a wide canopy and appear smooth on the surface with no manufactured lines or rivets. They have a gray or silver tone to them much like that of the element mercury or liquid aluminum. They are less brilliant than their coupled spheres and have a saucer or disc shape from the side. The admiral for the first time is without words, as it appears that he is looking at a flying saucer. As if that wasn't enough, these objects seem to morph into a boomerang shape with inverted wings and an elongated nose cone that is thin about three feet in width. These morphed spade fighters begin to move toward the constricted vesicle in the same grid pattern as the spheres. The admiral looks toward the now trivial Russians to see their reaction of the phenomenon that is taking place. His reason for concern falls on the fact that they have also sounded their battle station whistles and have once again taken aggressive formations. The admiral being the soldier he is calls in to the president to describe the nature of the moment.

"Terence, you need to see this. The ocean was glowing with all the colors of the rainbow. Then these spheres broke the surface in the thousands and were followed by these spade-type fighters that paired up to each orb. I have never seen shit like this in my life."

"Do not engage, Daniel. I think that whatever they are they are there to help," responds the president.

"You got it, but I'm not sure the Russians are on the same page."

Then with a long pause, the admiral seems to have a stutter to his voice, and the president asks, "What the matter?"

"Terence, this massive craft has now broke the surface and is headed toward the containment vesicle five hundred yards to my bow."

With some fear in his tone, he describes the ship as a "V"-shaped object about three stories in height. From tip to tip, he guesses at about fifteen football fields in width, and in the center mass of the "V" is another transparent sphere about three thousand feet in radius.

Aside from the water falling from the object back to the ocean, it too has no sound. Its color is different, more of an earth tone gray mimicking the ocean floor with shadows that give a false image of depth that camouflages the smooth, seamless lines of this magnificent craft. The admiral wonders how long that object has been here and why it hasn't been discovered before.

"It would have to have been seen by radar, anything the size of a small city would have to be," shouts the admiral.

The admiral calls to his man working the radar for verification. He reports that nothing shows on radar or any system from any of their ships, and the admiral truly feels he is dealing with an advanced species. Watching in astonishment, the admiral can't help but feel impressed; however, his adolescent admiration is cut short as the Russians fire at the massive object. The hovering fortress does nothing to avoid the incoming rounds fired from the Russian warships and continues its determined path to the targeted vesicle. As the rounds plaster the sky, it appears the fortress has a shimmering hue around it deflecting the direct rounds and avoiding any direct contact.

"A goddamn force field," shouts the admiral.

But in his amazement, he fails to notice the deflected rounds now head toward his fleet once again and now jeopardize all his sailors and civilians. With the aggressive tactics of the Russians, the spade fighters and their paired orbs break from their disciplined grid pattern swarming to the air and begin diving in on the command Russian ship. As aimless fire deflects off the descending spade fighters, non-targeted rounds continue to fall mere feet from the Atlantic US fleet. Forced to protect the sailors, the admiral orders the fleet to ready the weapon systems, as an engagement seems inevitable. With the tensions growing rapidly, the admiral waits to give the order to attack hoping for a non-violent resolve. It's then it seems his prayers are answered when the spade fighters unleash rapid bursts of concentrated energy rounds in several brilliant colors at the weapon systems of the Russian warship Frunze. The brilliant rounds light up the sky and mutilate the advanced weapon systems like they are made of paper. The Russians are now immobilized and defenseless realizing they are dealing with a more advanced species and cease firing with the few remaining active weapons. They all watch as the fortress hovers over the vesicle precisely positioning itself directly over the chaos.

The admiral relieved by the fact he averted another international incident orders all ships to report any damage from the Russian offensive. To his surprise, there was no damage to his fleet, but he is given disastrous news that a civilian ship full of volunteers was hit and completely destroyed. The admiral looks to the rear and sees scattered debris from the civilian vessel and orders for an immediate search of survivors. The news is given to the president who now understands the seriousness of not only an alien race in the Atlantic but also the international ramifications of an attacked civilian ship. President Anderson realizes the importance of his decision and orders the admiral to quickly recover any survivors of the wrecked volunteer ship but to stand fast and wait for further orders. It appears the president is more concerned with monitoring the alien crafts than dealing with an already aggressive adversary. The admiral acknowledges his orders and watches as the amazing landscape etches eternal memories of incomprehensible detail into a once accomplished mind. Life as of today is unfamiliar, and the admiral feels like a toddler first learning how to walk, but it's dwarfed by the understanding that this is just the beginning.

"Terence, there appears to be no survivors. We recovered as many bodies as we could. What would you like for me to do?" reports the admiral.

"Head home. These craft have begun to appear all over the world. I need you here as my advisor and my friend," answers the president.

With the turmoil behind them and uncertainty ahead, the US fleet sails toward the New York shores knowing only that this morning was the dawn of a new world.

Chapter 10

The fresh smell of cut grass riddles the air, and the comfortable tingle of the sun warms Vinny's face as he takes his seat behind the New York Yankees dugout. The crack of the bat has always been a melody that reminds him of his childhood as it is echoed throughout the stadium. The bases are loaded bottom of the ninth, and it's a tied game with only one out, and the stadium is going crazy as the teams' captain takes his place at the plate. Vinny filled with anticipation embraces the experience as one of life's distinguished moments but can't help but think something is missing. The answer to the mystery is solved as a vendor yells out, "Ice-cold beer here!"

Vinny grabs the coldest beer he could find and watches as the first pitch is thrown.

Strike!

The captain steps out as he takes a breath and prepares for the next pitch.

Strike!

The crowd starts to stand as the captain sits behind in the count; the pitcher eyes the catcher's mitt with confidence and throws a hard fastball for the strikeout trying to silence the crowd. The ball cuts to the inside but up and as if it was recorded in slow motion. Vinny sips his beer and watches as the ball meshes with the bat and is launched into the air. The intense brisk flavor of the beer rushes into his palate and is accented by the excitement of the ball heading toward the wall. Vinny raises his hands high above his head spilling the expendable beer on his lucky Yankee hat as he watches in amazement the winning ball clear the wall and the right fielder's glove.

"Home run. Home run. The Yankees win!" screams Vinny.

The large screen in center field replays the sensational hit as the captain rounds the bases and is met by his animated teammates gathered around home plate. Vinny can hardly contain himself and begins to look around to celebrate with someone. In that moment, the stadium seems stifled as Vinny notices he is sitting alone. He then tries to hear the announcer but finds it impossible as the once celebrating team stops and looks up at the sky. Vinny turns to the crowd behind him but realizes he is now alone in the stadium, and it begins to get cold, as the once revitalizing sun has disappeared. He stares again at the field and is shocked to see no players anywhere to speak of, and the now haunting stadium has become uncomfortable. The nightmare gets worse as the blackened sky begins to flash with lightning as it strikes the historic landmark and rain pours onto the field. Vinny watches helplessly as water covers the field, and the walls of the wonderful place begin to crumble from the repeated strikes of destructive lightning. Vinny is devastated as the walls topple around him as a wall of water rushes in devouring any remnants of the stadium. Vinny watches in astonishment as he is swept into the water-filled streets of New York where city skyscrapers are almost all covered by the annihilating water. The relentless water seems to continue to rise, and in moments, the city of New York becomes submerged, and no signs of its existence remain when he faintly hears someone call his name. As he stares around looking for the soft voice, he seems to be at the mercy of the monstrous flood, but then he sees in the distant Sophia calling out to him.

The conscious recognition of Sophia allows Vinny to realize the images of Yankees stadium were an unconscious dream brought on by the earlier blast. With his attention drawn to the obvious, he realizes that the ship, he, Sophia, and Ethan were on, was destroyed. As he looks around, he sees a debris field scattered all around him, and he makes way toward Sophia who has clung on to the larger part of the boat's hull. The cold Atlantic Ocean makes it hard to swim as he starts to lose feeling in his hands. With each stroke, the pain gets worse, but it is quickly interrupted by an unrecognizable landscape. Vinny stares at the once hypnotic vesicle that earlier demanded his attention and watches as it's replaced by swarms of orbs, unrecognizable shaped craft, and a massive fortress that has begun to engulf it. Though the magnificent scene is almost mesmerizing, Vinny maintains his determination in reaching the frightened Sophia. As he gets closer, he sees the determined face of Sophia as she yells out for Ethan. Vinny reaches out to the large piece of debris and hoists himself next to the emotional Sophia.

"What is going on? What are all those things flying around?" asks Sophia.

"I don't know, but they're not from here. They are way more advanced than anything I have seen on Earth," replies Vinny.

Vinny wraps his arms around the shivering Sophia and scans the debris field looking for Ethan. A few feet behind them they hear a melodious moan, and they rush to see Ethan floating on his back in inexpressible pain. Without any hesitation, Vinny leaps into the frigid waters and wraps up Ethan in his arms and slowly brings him onto the now crowded debris. Once on board, they notice that Ethan is bleeding from his mouth and ears, and he has begun to shiver uncontrollably. Sophia who has some limited experience in first aid knows this is the sign of shock and possible internal bleeding.

"We need to get him medical attention quick," says Sophia.

With the riotous atmosphere all around, they only see the distant images of the US fleet, the uninviting Russian's, and the arcane objects that have inherited the sky. They realize the chances are slim that anyone even notices them and that the likely hood of a rescue to be unrealistic. Sophia nestles up to Ethan and throws her arm over to a distraught Vinny and says, "We need to keep warm. If we huddle together, we can use our body heat."

"What about Ethan?" asks Vinny.

"Let's make this as comfortable as possible for him, but there is a good chance he won't make it," says Sophia in an emotional tone.

"I'm glad you're here, Sophia," responds Vinny as he too embraces his friends and tries to keep them warm.

They continue to watch as the massive "V"-shaped fortress devours the entire vesicle as it begins to slowly make way below the surface. The scattered crafts have now changed to a crescent moon-type configuration still paired up with the orbs and have taken to the skies almost blocking the sun like a massive flock of birds. As the last of the fortress vanishes below the once trauma-tized area of the ocean, the now crescent moon-shaped object and their orbs descend at incredible speeds toward the same waters. As these objects impact the ocean, they change shape once again to an aerodynamic-shaped fighter and enter the water with absolutely no sound or splash. Thousands of objects penetrate the waters around them, and in moments, there are no signs of the mystifying events that unfolded.

Several hundred yards away, they watch as the US fleet con-tinues to get more distant leaving them with a hopeless outlook of any rescue and an eerie feeling of gloom. Vinny looks again to the area where the vesicle had disappeared into the abyss and sees only a landscape of a Russian fleet whose attentions seem to have turned in their direction. Sophia and Vinny find some contentment in the frightening Russian fleet in that they may be their only hope. Ethan, who seems to be getting worse, howls out unnerving cries forcing Vinny and Sophia to try their best to get the Russians' attention. In the horizon, they watch as a smaller craft heads in their direction coming from the Russian fleet, and they become overwhelmed with excitement as they realize that they are going to be rescued.

"I'm sure they have medical officers on board," says Sophia.

"I'm sure they do. We need to just keep Ethan calm and warm. It's gonna be a while till that small boat gets here," responds Vinny.

"So what do you make of all those things and the way they cleaned up the mess?" asks Sophia.

"What I do know is that they aren't man-made. I sometimes get caught up in the TV shows that Ethan watches, and there has always been a connection between the ocean and UFOs," answers Vinny.

"Until now, I never believed in aliens or UFOs. I even some-times wonder if God exists. It's like we are prisoners to ignorance and religions," says Sophia.

Vinny for years has been in deep studies of religion and wants to avoid any controversial conversation with Sophia over something she may not understand. To avoid an issue, he only says one quote that relates to several years of research and his studies.

"It's not God in question but religion. The world isn't a prison house but a kind of spiritual kindergarten where millions of bewildered infants are trying to spell God with all the wrong blocks. The only thing we can guarantee in life is that there are no guarantees. As far as I'm concerned, there couldn't be more of a case in point than right now," answers Vinny.

With the small boat getting closer, Sophia absorbs the comments from Vinny and smirks to acknowledge the intelligent rebuttal to her emotional defiance of a careless comment in which she has no idea about. She grips his arm with a hint of both compassion and attraction perhaps brought on by extenuating circumstance but affection nonetheless. Together, they stand up to welcome the small boat that now drifts only fifty yards away. It's then they realize things aren't exactly what they thought it was going to be.

Chapter 11

The Russian fleet rest in amazement as the pride of their group sits incapacitated after being riddled with the alien firepower. Their crew watches as the US fleet sails back toward there shores, worried of the outcome from there careless assault on the alien craft that left a US civilian ship destroyed. The commanding officer calls Moscow for advisement and to avoid a conflict with an American fleet that now has an edge due to the Russian fleet being crippled.

"Sir, the firepower was precise and dynamic. It resisted our ammunitions effortlessly reflecting them like light on a mirror," says the officer.

"Where are they now?" asks Moscow.

"Gone, sir. In less than five minutes thousands of vessels dove below the surface along with the massive craft that absorbed the contaminating event," responds the officer.

"Are there any casualties to your crew?" asks Moscow.

"Negative, sir. Their weapons hit with surgical precision only affecting our weapon systems, but our fire did damage a US civilian ship," answers the Russian officer.

"Were there any survivors?" asks Moscow.

"We watched as the US fleet pulled bodies from the ravaged ship's debris field. They sailed off with no aggression focused on us," responds the officer.

"Plausible deniability is our case. Scan the wreckage, and if you find any survivors, destroy them," demands Moscow.

"Yes, sir. We are launching a small gunship now," answers the officer.

"Stand by with the fleet. Reports around the world match the objects you encountered. We need to consult with the prime minister as to how we need to respond to this possible threat," replies Moscow.

The aft of the command ship opens, revealing a heavily gunned ship that takes to the water and heads in the direction of scattered debris. The commanding officer aboard the small gunboat looks through his binoculars searching for any signs of life. His crew is distressed by the past events and is anxious to get back to their ship begging the officer to turn around. The officer though known for his heroism considers their plea as the ocean beneath him still glows of brilliant colors and noticeable objects scurry around just under the waterline. Maintaining his discipline, he continues to search the debris when he spots three civilians clinging to a large piece of the demolished ship's hull. He orders the crew to lock and load their weapons and prepares them for his orders to fire. Several minutes later, the gunship now drifts five hundred yards away, and the officer can see that one of the civilians is hurt and that the other two may be all that's left of their concern. With the officer still concerned for the safety of himself and his crew, he orders them to fire outside the range of their gun's accuracy.

"Ogon!" shouts the officer.

With the command, the crew opens fire and riddles the area with a hail of bullets dousing the debris with water from the inaccurate rounds.

Vinny watches the boat come hard to port and stares as what appears to be large flashes come from the powerful guns mounted on the small ship.

"They're firing at us!" shouts Sophia.

The water begins to soak them as the rounds hit only feet in front of the vulnerable debris they cling to. The vicious sounds of murderous guns get louder as the gunship closes in accelerating the accuracy and the chances of a kill. Vinny won't leave Ethan or Sophia and can only shield them as bullets begin to splinter the wood around them. Sophia begins to cry uncontrollably as she begins to pray to the God she once questioned. Vinny knowing he offers no safety embraces his friends to offer only comfort. Vinnie's body gets tight with anticipation of the murderous rounds, as the deafening cracks of the guns seem to be directly behind him. Vinny once again closes his eyes and remembers his dream of a day at the ballpark and begins to smile embracing his fate. Before the smell of the fresh-cut grass could enter his consciousness, he is brought to reality by silence. Confused Vinny turns over his shoulder still shielding his friends and watches as a milky bubble encases them. The Russian gunship still determined continues to fire, but Vinny can't hear the disturbing pop from the bloodthirsty guns and sees only the bullets striking the bubble causing a ripple effect like a stone on a pond. Vinny lightly taps the frightened Sophia to appease his sanity as the once brisk December ocean air is replaced by comforting warmth. Sophia turns and watches as she too is confused by the rapid change of events. The welcome bubble has now completely engulfed them, and the aggressive gunship has ceased fire and has forced it to head back toward the Russian fleet. With the revitalizing environment surrounding them, Vinny and Sophia stand up to watch the attacking gunship sail away. As they stand there and stare, they are jolted back by a silent explosive blast of water outside the bubble that annihilates the once threatening gunship. They shield their eyes out of instinct and quickly redirect their attention back outside the bubble.

The ocean has become alive with colorful lights, and thousands of the orbs and now definite fighters have taken to the noon air. They stare again into the entrancing sky as the crafts hover hundreds of feet above them in a grid-like pattern darkening the skies as far as they could see. Sophia turns behind her as she hears a slight hum and feels a vibration rattle off the splintered debris she has grown accustomed to. She stares at a larger disc-shaped craft breaking the surface only a few feet behind them. She taps Vinny on the shoulder that remains engrossed by the crafts filling the noon skies. As the disc-shaped craft elevates above them, Sophia grabs Vinny with a bit more aggression forcing him to be aware of the object that now hovers over them. With Vinny now distant from his hypnotic trance of the amazing grid, he focuses on the disc and its brilliant light above him that has lowered itself around the milky bubble. The disc centers itself on the bubble giving it a vintage UFO image and begins to descend giving full view of the ocean world below. In astonishment, Sophia and Vinny watch as they see an entire ocean floor alive with exotic craft ranging from small to enormous. They are awestruck by the speeds and turns of these crafts, as well as the sheer multitude that has now begun to inhabit the obvious mysteries of the world below. Before they can endure the magnitude of such inconceivable ideas, Ethan yells out in excruciating pain reminding the bewildered duo of their injured friend helpless and scared.

"Hold on, Ethan. I have a feeling you're gonna be okay," says Sophia.

"Bro, you wouldn't believe this. It's like I'm watching one of your shows in 3D. If there is anyone who can help you, it's got to be these guys," says Vinny.

The disc has begun to increase its speed, but it has no effect on any of the three inside. They weave in and out of the countless objects that control the ocean floor breaking through to expose a wide trench. The trench is deep and dark, and with a swift movement, they dive into its heart going miles below any point in which man has been able to. Vinny is amazed at the fact there has been no pressure felt or uneasiness from the rapid movement of the highly maneuverable craft that controls them. The lights of the distant alien inhabitants fade, and they find themselves in the dark; their conscious feeling is that they are still descending at incredible speeds but have no way of knowing how fast or where they're headed. In the distance, a shimmer of light breaks from the suspicious dark revealing a possible end to their journey.

"Hold on, Sophia. I think we are going to break through and into that light," says Vinny.

And in that moment, the once small hint of light becomes a magnificent conduit and opens to a world beneath the world exposing miles of intelligent life. There before them is a race within our world that must have been here as long as us to make something so grand. They see a beautiful city filled with elaborate transit systems and majestic buildings littered with translucent colors all in harmony. Yet among the progressive buildings, you see camouflaged structures of ancient past resembling pyramids and mystical statues that once populated the land above.

"It's beautiful and comforting. It almost feels like we are home or at nana's house," says Sophia.

Vinny chuckles at the analogy and continues to gawk at the lustrous landscape and can't help but feel he is beginning a new chapter in his once mediocre life.

"I never would have guessed this is how my day would have went," giggles Vinny.

"Went? I think our day has just begun," answers Sophia.

As they watch their bubble slow down and head into this estranged city, they see a monumental building that demands attention and appears to be the essential hub in which all points meet. Its size is magnificent and would dwarf any building seen before in the world above. As they close in on the building, they see an opening revealing a tender teal glow that the bubble seems to direct itself into. Within moments, they find themselves inside the city walls, and the once tender glow is replaced with troubled darkness. Vinny grabs Sophia's hand offering comfort in a difficult situation as they anticipate the theatre that has become their life.

Chapter **12**

As the admiral's ship pulls into the New York Bay harbor, he can't help but stare at the thousands of disciplined crafts that now hold their grid pattern high above the city's landscape. The docks are filled with hundreds of reporters hoping to get the scoop on the breaking story and violently demand a statement from the drained-looking admiral as he leaves his ship.

"No comment. We know nothing of the situation or the entity that has presented itself," states the admiral.

"Are they a threat? What defense are we prepared to take?" shouts one reporter.

"If they were a threat, I believe they would have attacked already, and I refuse to consider any defense to an entity that already saved millions of lives," responds the admiral.

The reporters go ballistic with the comment demanding an explanation on how they have saved millions of lives. In the distance, the reporters focus on the hoard of media that now make way off the Lexington II hoping that some professional courtesy may give them closure. The admiral takes advantage of the distraction and heads toward Marine One that waits to take him to Washington. Once on board, he is surrounded by comfort, from the plush leather seats and appetizing snacks and drinks to the convenient technology of flat-screen monitors and the most up-to-date media players. As the helicopter lifts off, the admiral is embarrassed by his appearance and the marks of residue left on anything he touches. A medic continues to bandage his burnt arm and work on some bleeding gashes from his head that continue to soak his tattered uniform. The admiral closes his eyes knowing the flight to Washington will take a while by helicopter but is kept awake by the echoing noise reflected off of the city's buildings.

"Captain, why are we flying so low and through the city and not above it?" asks the admiral.

"Sorry sir, but if we get above the buildings our gauges go crazy. The crafts seem to emit an Electronic Magnetic pulse discharge that fry any electronic devise" responds the pilot.

"EMPs. Is it intentional?" asks the admiral.

"I don't think so, sir. It seems to be an energy disbursed by the aliens.

"Has Washington made it official they are aliens?" asks the admiral.

"Everything indicates we are the aliens, sir. I have Washington on the line now," answers the pilot.

The comment from the pilot perplexes the admiral but disregards it as a misunderstanding and begins talking with the president.

"Hey, Daniel. It's Terence. I wanna brief you on what we know. I know you're tired and hurt, but I need your help," says the president.

"I understand. I'll be fine. Give me some details," says the admiral.

One of the officers hands the admiral a laptop that has a remote connection to the president's reports. After some security verification and passwords, the computer screen becomes alive with reports and images of the present situation.

"Okay, Daniel, here is what we have. The satellite shots show the grid is worldwide. The images you see are inferred, and they have no heat signatures," says the president.

"So they could be unmanned," responds the admiral.

"Or they may have a way to cloak themselves, but you see the orbs? They may be a power source. There is one orb per craft but when they move they move like bolt lightning, showcasing an immense amount of controlled energy," says the president.

"I see the close-ups of them. The orbs are like mirrors, but the crafts next to them are dull almost liquid-like. What have they displayed so far?" asks the admiral.

"You are 100 percent correct. They can modify their shape at will, but they currently have a crescent moon shape with a long tail or nose cone. As I'm sure, the pilots told you they emit a small EMP discharge and have a heavy magnetic charge to them. One Middle Eastern state fired on the craft assuming it was one of ours. The report showed that whatever they fired was reflected away exposing a shimmer outside the craft and orb, kind of like a force field. Even though they were provoked, they still didn't attack," says the president.

"Yeah, I witnessed this firsthand. The vesicle that contained the accident was fired on along with the fortress that consumed it. All the weapons fired reflected off that shield, but at one point, they did retaliate and fire highly concentrated energy rounds at the Russians with surgical precision disabling their entire weapon system, so rest assured they could be aggressive," responds the admiral.

"I understand, but as of now, we have no reason to think they have hostile intentions. I'm sending you now the Pacific and Atlantic reports that show the activity via satellite. The ocean is alive, Daniel, and they outnumber us as an estimate twenty to one, and I don't mean the USA. I mean us the entire human race. I'm also sending some other reports on both history and the ocean revolving around the phenomenon called USOs," says the president.

"Some of these objects are miles in diameter. It's amazing. The reports are indicating that some of these as you put it "spade-type fighters" are traveling at over three hundred knots. That kind of technology is years away for us. We just started to understand supercavitation," says the admiral.

"Daniel, the reports show that some of the deepest points in the ocean are over thirty-five thousand feet. On average, the oceans are just over two miles in depth. That's a lot of room to hide. Hell, 70 percent of this planet is ocean and only 10 percent has been explored. For years, we have spent millions on space exploration when the most alien world is our own," replies the president.

"The reports around USO history seem speculative at best but nonetheless interesting. The reports go back to Christopher Columbus and straight into an explosion of sightings around World War II. Even with today's technology, most reports are vague from creditable people like military pilots and officers at sea. I can't help but think that there has to be some kind of cover-up from generation to generation," says the admiral.

"What I'm sending you now is classified. These are the pages of project blue book that were left out of the public file. This shows reports from Roswell to area fifty-one, as well as high-definition video from the air force. I believe the cover-up was an attempt to harness the technology and keep other nation's eyes away, but we failed to ever get close to an alien craft other than crashes. My largest concern comes from a naval base off the coast of Bermuda and the countless reports from the Bermuda triangle. I have numerous reports showing evidence of possible micro-wormholes under the sea in the area of the Bermuda coast. The theory of a wormhole indicates interdimensional travel allowing alien craft to come and go as they please without ever entering any air space," reveals the president.

"My only thought to that, Terence, is that these entities have been here a long time. I only base that on the historical reports showing influence going back as early as primitive man. That idea is based only on cave painting and carvings, but it gets more detailed as we became more civilized. The history of influence is heavy in the time of ancient Egypt and the time of Christ. The Bible is written with primitive thought and can be easily misinterpreted that an alien craft or being is a god rather than a more advanced species. The concept could be the answer to the proverbial missing link and could explain the nature of our very existence," speculates the admiral.

"Get some rest when you get here. We will indulge in theories, but as of now, I'm convinced that we consider only a peaceful approach and do what we can to make some kind of contact," answers the president.

"You got it, Terence. I will see you soon. My head is killing me," says the admiral.

And as they stop communication, the admiral stares around the helicopter and sees nothing but wide-eyed officers itching to hear more of the ideas revolving around a possible alien species.

"Everyone here has top security clearance so I wanna discuss a few things with you to get some opinions," asks the admiral.

All the personnel onboard agree, and the admiral begins to search the Internet opening conspiracy sites and top-visited UFO and alien Web pages. He also compares them to the classified information given to him by the president.

"These sites have all been written off as absurd ideologies generated by simpletons and have been debated by scientists with PhDs from Harvard to local community colleges. Till today, I was a skeptic to say the least, but considering the consistencies, similar objects and beings, sight locations, and ancient folklore, I would have to disagree with those skeptics. If I type Bible and UFO into any search engine, I'm riddled with sites that show passage after passage quoted out of the Bible that can be interpreted as alien. The images of ancient statues and tapestries showing saucer-shaped objects in the sky thousands of years before flight were invented or thought about. There are pages of video and pictures from civilian and military personnel of unexplained craft followed by hundreds of critics flashing their expertise on how they are images of weather balloons or signal flares. Today is a day most humbling for those people and an awakening for the people of this world," states the admiral.

"Sir, even project blue book can't explain 7 percent beyond the weather balloons and signal flares. Ancient folklore is written off as well, due to the idea they believed in sun gods and other mythologies. I don't want to stand for ignorance, but we can't assume the idea of aliens without the idea of Zeus or Neptune," says one of the officers.

"Lieutenant commander, I appreciate your thought, but we don't have Zeus hovering a thousand feet above us right now. I also would consider the thought that the very idea of those primitive concepts may be based on the inability to understand a more advanced life-form and their technologies," answers the admiral.

"Admiral, not to change the paths of thought, but why help us now? Especially if they have been here since the dawn of time?" asks the pilot.

"Why do you feel they have been here since the dawn of time? We have no evidence of that fact, and the concept of wormholes indicates they could come and go as they please without any detection," asks the admiral.

"With all due respect, Admiral, history and science has been battling with the people who research UFO evidence and conspiracies. Science proves that we evolved from primates, but science comes to a halt between the Neanderthal and an intelligent civilization. Research shows a chimp can construct basic tools to extract food. Sir, we built pyramids and established government. If that isn't a sign of outside influence, what is?" responds the pilot.

The helicopter's crew and passengers grow silent as the admiral ponders the pilot's point. After a few unsettling seconds, the admiral laughs to himself and reaches over tapping the pilot's shoulder in recognition.

"You make a great argument, son, and I'm sure I don't have a rebuttal. Let's get to Washington. I'm sure they're trying to convince the president to fire a nuclear missile by now," remarks the admiral.

The crew is amused from the sign of humor by the admiral considering all that he has endured in the last twenty-four hours.

Dusk has begun to creep over Washington, and warm shades of orange hug the horizon darkening the silhouette of the nation's capital. Marine One comes to rest on the White House lawn, and several well-armed marines rush to meet the admiral as he exits the helicopter. The president stands at the edge of the lawn eager to greet his longtime friend with a fresh-pressed uniform and aspirin.

"Good to see you. You look like shit. I got leaders of countries I didn't even know existed calling me for advisement. I have all world leaders headed to the UN by December 11, which gives me a few days to figure out how we plan on communicating with the entity," says the president.

The admiral grabs the aspirin and his uniform and heads into the White House showing signs of fatigue as he acknowledges what his friend tells him.

"Sounds like a plan. I had some good conversation with the flight crew, and they had some great points of view. I wanna get some rest, and we will meet up in the early morning and brainstorm on how we may want to communicate with them. This is a delicate situation, and I want to make sure my head is right. Thanks for the uniform and aspirin. I will see you in the morning," says the admiral.

"The house is yours. Anything you need, Daniel. I will post a guard outside your door and make it clear that you're not disturbed," answers back the president.

The two friends shake hands and smirk before going their separate ways. The president stops and stares at the rapidly approaching night sky that now looks so unfamiliar as its filled with more than stars. For the first time, the sky reflects a new face, and for the first time, the once recognizable sky now looks alien.

Chapter 13

The room is exceptionally dark and eerie as Vinny and Sophia begin to feel constrained. Neither one of them will move continuing the uncomfortable silence echoing throughout their subconscious. Vinny feeling unsettled yells out in a heavy New York accent hoping to get some sort of response.

"Hello, is anyone there? We have a man hurt, and he needs medical attention."

Vinnie's comment still rings around the darkened room as it's accented by a nervous whimper expressed from a frightened Sophia. Vinny leans toward Sophia as the comfortless room lightens into a revealing teal glow. The room is bare and smooth with no signs of lines separating the walls from the floor. With the now absent bubble no longer confining them, Vinny is able to touch the surface that resembles a fresh waxed car but is confused by the foamy texture. Ethan has begun to shake and sweat uncontrollably forcing Sophia to rush to his aid. Vinny forces himself to focus on his friend and to disregard the unfamiliar surroundings encompassing them. Vinny becomes overwhelmed with anticipation and concern and in a frantic tone tries to yell once again only to be interrupted by a distinct light, giving promise to an exit. As the light's brilliance blinds them, it exposes an outline of a large doorway accenting several silhouettes of beings unknown. Fear rips through Vinny and Sophia regarding the intentions of the beings, yet they huddle around Ethan with no mind for their own safety. The cool teal glow gets brighter as the doorway closes behind the beings shedding light on the once blackened silhouettes. Vinny stands tall welcoming any fate as Sophia continues to comfort Ethan. The beings begin to walk slowly toward them as they seem equally unsure of either's reaction.

"There are eight of them, but I can't make anything out. I can't tell if they are human or not, but I will make sure they don't hurt you," says Vinny in a low tone trying to accent his character.

"It looks like they are walking on two legs and have arms. They got to be human. This is some secret military base that conducts illegal experiments on people and animals. Watch," says Sophia.

"Don't start, Sophia. The *Tyrannosaurus rex* stood on two feet and had two arms, and it was far from human," responds Vinny.

Silenced by the witty comment, Sophia continues to brush Ethan's hair with her fingers whispering spirited words of encouragement as the beings continue in their direction. As the uncertain group converges, their appearance becomes evident and detailed, as it's clear they are not human. As if the introduction to an advanced species isn't enough, their presence though exotic feels somewhat familiar. Their appearances aren't the same as two are different from the rest. The two beings in the center of the group seem older or wiser. The taller one looks like a bald old man with countless years and experience mapping his facial skeleton. His eyes are black and sunken dwarfed by the large sockets that are shaped like small footballs. His skull is oversized and deep, sheathed in dense skin resembling the tough hide of a rhinoceros. His ears are slightly pink and familiar; they too are oversized and look much like a human's. His nose seems to be a pit with red and pink filters and a split that runs only inches from his mouth. The mouth and jaw are drawn back with no sign of a chin, and his lips seem tight following the lines of a permanent frown. His high cheekbones, oversized skull, and sunken eyes fitted by the rugged, grayish, and hairless skin give him character to the retro alien introduced in the early twentieth century. His torso seems delicate yet tight with long arms and similar tough skin. His hands have three long fingers with fingernails that seem like bone, and they touch just below the knee. The rest is hidden by a semi-sheer cloak draping over the delicate body and clasped at the waist. To his right is a similar alien smaller in height yet sharing his presence and experiences. The other six have comparable attributes of the center two, but they are of a different nature. They share the rugged tight grayish skin and elongated skull but are more generic than the other two. Their skulls are marked by a row of short horns or spikes traveling from one ear to the other and down the center. Their eyes fill the football-shaped sockets and are accented by the aggressive brow. They have a small pit for a nose with a flap of dense cartilage covering the center with a running split short of their upper lip. Their lips and mouth are tight but much like that of a human centered on a strong-looking jawline. They have longer necks that run to a sculpted frame of muscle and rawhide skin. Their arms are strong and defined ending with large three-fingered powerful hands. The tip of each finger seems to have a bone or nail that extends two or three inches and is thick giving an aggressive vibe to menacing creature. They have no distinctive genitals and continue their convincing muscle tone into their thighs and calves finished by an aggressive clubfoot anchored by three wide bone spikes. Their appearance is aggressive, yet they do not carry the look of wisdom and experience of the other two. They seem like a limited life-form harvested to be the caretakers of the other beings, an expendable clone genetically created from the others to serve.

"My name is Vinny. This is Sophia and our friend Ethan who is hurt. Can you help us?" opens Vinny.

The aliens begin to shuffle around with two of the aggressive-looking creatures focusing on Ethan. From the floor, a flat slab emerges and hovers only inches from the ground. The two aliens begin to tend to Ethan trying to move him delicately onto the hovering board. Sophia who has been nursing Ethan remains watchful as the aliens take out an instrument that seems to scan the severity of Ethan's injuries.

"It's okay, Sophia. Let them help him," says Vinny.

The hovering board lifts Ethan a few feet from the floor with the aliens standing at each side. They glance over at the older two as if receiving orders and nod their heads in compliance. Vinny watches as the aliens stand patiently by Ethan, and the two older ones in front of them turn and stare at Vinny and Sophia. Vinny hears a voice echo around him, and he quickly turns trying to find its source.

"Here in front of you," says the voice.

Vinny confused stares at the two entities that seem to almost gaze beyond them.

"Who is talking to me? I can't see anyone talking," asks Vinny.

"We are. Don't be alarmed. You are not in danger," says the voice.

Vinny realizes the voice is in fact the two older aliens that stand before him, and they are communicating with telepathy. Vinny uncomfortable with someone in his head asks politely if they could talk out loud.

"My name is Amun. This is my son Yhovah. Your friend is bleeding internally, and if he doesn't get medical attention, he will die. Please follow us," says the alien out loud.

The board carrying Ethan begins to move as the aliens on each side keep pace. Amun and his son walk ahead of them, while the remaining aggressive aliens surround them as if being protected. Vinny and Sophia follow in tow as another door opens exposing the radical world of the alien city inhabiting the ocean floor. The hall is clear exposing the illuminated city and the array of creatures that dwell at the deepest points of the ocean. Fish scatter as an enormous squid mentioned in fairytales darts between them trailing layers of black ink. Sophia keeps pace with the group, but Vinny begins to fall behind marveling at all the life around him. Sophia and the group are several yards ahead and out of sight of Vinny who scrambles to catch up. As Vinny turns around, he walks into a large chamber that is transparent and houses thousands of pods that are ringed with advanced monitors resembling something out of a video arcade. Each pod has one of the worker aliens inside of it, and the pods flash soft pastel colors making the room hypnotic. Each monitor is seamless giving the pod a three-hundred-sixty-degree view of some-thing. Vinny leans in forcing his eyes to focus beyond the lights and onto the monitors that reveal views of the world above. Vinny who throughout his life has been a video game fanatic compares it to a flight simulator and becomes captivated by its purpose. Vinny yet again getting sidetracked tries to move in closer, but before he can get too far, he hears Sophia call is name.

"What the hell are you doing?" asks Sophia.

"I want to know what those pods are. There has to be thousands of them. You can almost see through them and its looks like they have controls inside. It's got to be a simulator," says Vinny.

"Not for nothing, but Ethan is waiting on you in a room across the hall. Your fascination with the pods can wait. I bet you have an Xbox or something at home, don't you?" says Sophia.

Snapping back into the moment, Vinny rushes out to the hall with Sophia where they are met by another alien. This alien is tiny maybe two feet in height and looks more like a human. He has smooth skin and larger eyes but with a distinctive nose and mouth paired with a sense of innocence.

"He looks like a child," says Sophia.

"He seems more human than the rest, like a hybrid," responds Vinny.

The young alien giggles and takes off, while Vinny and Sophia watch him sprint into another open doorway.

"This way," says a voice as Sophia and Vinny make way toward the open door where Ethan waits. They enter a room that is bright white with a smooth surface where Ethan rests on the hovering board.

"It smells like Band-Aids in here, and what's up with those rings?" asks Vinny.

The two aliens who have escorted Ethan continue to move the board in through the center of the three rings and move away as the room turns from bright white to a pink tinge.

"Is it safe?" whispers Sophia.

"It better be," says Vinny.

Amun rests his hand on Vinnie's shoulder and asks him to step back from the rings as they slowly begin to rotate. Each ring rotates opposite the other and begins to rock back and forth forcing the rings to continually touch. The movement becomes so rapid that the rings begin to blur and Ethan appears to be encased in a tunnel. A blue or green glow lights up around Ethan, and a holographic image of Ethan begins to etch directly above him.

"That's disgusting. It's showing all his insides," says Sophia.

"It's like an X-ray and MRI. I'm curious to see how it's going to fix him," says Vinny.

With the image becoming very detailed, red flashes on the hologram pinpoint the damaged areas of Ethan's body. As the red flash continues, the hologram begins to drop and integrate with Ethan

maintaining the locations of his injuries. The glow turns to a purple, and several robotic arms appear from the fast-moving rings
and begin to work on Ethan targeting the flashing red lights. Ethan
moves around and appears uncomfortable but not in pain as slowly
the flashing red lights disappear.

"It's fixing him. He seems to be getting some color," says Sophia.

After about an hour, the room regains its pink tinge, and the
rings begin to slow down revealing a healthy Ethan. Amun walks
over to the resting Ethan and scans over his body with a handheld
device.

"Your friend is 100 percent. We even repaired a heart con-
dition that would have caused him to pass in about forty years.
He will need to rest for a while. You can wait for him in the room
across the hall. I'm sure you have several questions as do we. When
your friend wakes, we will all have our chances to talk and get
acquainted," says Amun.

Sophia and Vinny are escorted across the hall by three of the
grunt aliens exposing even more of the mysterious city. The halls are
lined with ancient artifacts and different points of human culture
presenting the idea that they have been here for some time. Vinny
and Sophia enter the room prepared for them and find it's filled with
many luxuries. A large round bed filled with pillows marks the center,
and a table stocked with assorted fruits, fish, and meats rests against
the distant wall. A large video screen takes up most of the front wall
and plays continual news reports of the happenings above. The room
is decorated with statues of ancient kings and tapestries of untold stories of history past. It appears comfortable and for a moment allows
them to relax and take in all that has transpired. Sophia begins to sob
as she allows herself to unwind becoming emotional.

"It's okay, Sophia. Everything will be fine. Why don't you get
some rest or get something to eat," asks Vinny.

Sophia agrees and walks over to the fresh fruit and nibbles on
some grapes and chunks of melon, while Vinny lies down on the
cozy-looking bed. Sophia relaxes next to him sharing some fruit, and
soon, the two fall asleep catching up on some much-needed rest.

Chapter 14

The cool December air rushes around the White House putting an icy shell on the fallen snow. The dawn brings a slight orange glow to the morning sky filled with silhouettes of the stubborn alien crafts that remain in their stable grid. The president sips on his hot coffee from his favorite mug that reads world's greatest dad and stares out at the mystery-filled sky. The oval office door opens as the admiral walks in and sits; he is tired but eager to begin the day.

"Okay, Terence, so what's the agenda?" asks the admiral.

"This is my favorite time of day, Daniel, so calm, the virgin sky giving birth to a new day of promise or disappointment. Today, Daniel is different. This day is filled already with confusion, anticipation, and fear lingering from yesterday giving no room for promise or contentment," answers the president.

"This day begins a new era. This morning is the first morning that forces us to realize there are bigger things than our misguided ideas," says the admiral.

"Maybe you're right, or this sky could be inviting the end, the end of time, life, or ignorance but nonetheless the end," responds the president.

"I won't argue change. These things are way above my understanding. Their crafts are fast and powerful, and they out man us. They have fortresses that hover without sound that could house maybe two hundred thousand. Our oceans have become alive and could hide millions more of them undetected. From a military point of view, we are sitting ducks, but from a personal perspective, I don't feel threatened," points out the admiral.

"My biggest fear is outside reactions. I can control our actions, but we have no control of what other nations do. In the Middle East, there are reports showing extremist groups that are firing rockets at the crafts. The North Koreans are preparing a defense by positioning their long-range ballistic missiles on their shores. We need to convene together with all leaders and present a unified front and find a resolve as peaceful as we can," says the president.

"I think the best thing to do is address the nation, Terence. You have millions of frightened Americans out there. They need to know they have support," says the admiral.

The president nods his head in agreement and turns to an advisor asking him to make it so.

"What in the world do I say to millions of scared Americans when I don't even know the answers, and I'm just as scared?" says the president.

"Say what makes you, Terence, the truth, nothing rehearsed. Shoot from the hip but be sincere," responds the admiral.

The two sit up and begin to walk out of the oval office and head toward the media room where they have begun to set up for the president's address. Before they enter the room, the president turns and touches the admiral on the shoulder and says, "Thanks, Daniel. I'm glad you're here."

As he enters, several assistants swarm him with degrees from every Ivy League school advising him on the approach he should take. The president looks through them all and smiles at the admiral and shrugs them off as he stands at the podium and gets ready for his speech.

"My fellow Americans, I stand before you a scared and humbled man. This great nation has endured centuries of war, turmoil, and ignorance, not just abroad but here on our own soil as well. Throughout history, each time we have fallen on our faces, we have got up refusing to dust ourselves off and pressed on. We as a nation have become stronger each time making us proud to be Americans. Today marks maybe our largest challenge yet, to see that our world (sighs), yes our world, now bears witness to the unexplained, and I can't tell you who they are or what they want. In the centuries before, we allowed our ignorances to control our actions, causing riots and segregation that lead to chaos and a divided nation. I will not allow that same ignorances to surface on yet another prejudice idea. The crafts you see above your work, homes, and oceans have shown no sign of being hostile, and this nation will not provoke or entertain any action against these visitors. I ask that we as Americans regardless of other nation's actions remain civilized and maintain ourselves with the same regard that make this nation great. I will not harm the American people or allow anyone to harm you. Have faith in me as a father and husband not just your president that any actions done are with your families and mine in my thoughts and prayers. In a few days, I will meet with all the nations' leaders in NY and try as a unified group to present a peaceful solution. Until then, may God bless you and your families, and pray that our world may come together as one."

Chapter 15

Vinny begins to shuffle curling his legs into a comfortable fetal position; his eyes barely open, the room is blurry due to the fact his body refuses to wake up. As his eyes begin to focus, he realizes he has snuggled up to Sophia and smiles as he notices their arms meshed together.

"What are you smiling about?" asks Sophia.

"The banter of racism and how ridiculous it really is," replies Vinny as he notices the trivial skin tone difference between his arm and Sophia's.

"What do you mean? That is a major problem in the world, and I'm not sure that issue is resolved," answers Sophia.

"I guess that's my point, all those years of racial separation and hate controlling us, not just black and white but Muslims and Jews and any other prejudice. All those wasted years when true diversity lived miles below our oceans. I wonder if we would have shit on each other so much if we knew how much we were alike?" responds Vinny.

Sophia smiles and begins to rub Vinnie's arms as if to embrace his revelation. Vinny looks around the room reminding him of the unfamiliar surroundings and sits himself up. Feeling refreshed, he begins to walk around looking at the hundreds of ancient artifacts that overcast the smooth walls and floors that house them. The room has a unique vibe, like an old library filled with ancient books that house centuries of brilliance. Vinny marvels at the detailed tapestries and intricate lines of the numerous statues, while Sophia seems more reluctant to get out of the bed. Vinny stares at a large statue of a woman looking over her shoulder and a casket-shaped box accented with gold and begins to tear as he rubs a rustic pair of wood beams riddled with tattered ropes and rusted nails.

"Why are you crying?" asks Sophia as she walks over to Vinny for comfort.

"Do you know what this is? Do you know who that woman is looking at me or that box and most of all these beams of wood?" says Vinny with a small break in his voice.

"Leave it to you to think the woman is looking at you," jokes Sophia.

"Sophia, this is Lot's wife from the story of Sodom and Gomorrah, and this is the arc of the covenant, and this must be the cross they crucified Christ on!" shouts Vinny.

"Like Indiana Jones?" asks Sophia.

"Are you fucking kidding me?" shouts Vinny, before covering his mouth realizing his foul language around such holy relics.

"Nope, she isn't joking," replies a voice from the far corner.

"I know that sarcasm anywhere. Ethan, where are you?" says Vinny.

From around several other ancient relics surfaces Ethan looking refreshed and full of life. Sophia rushes over and hugs him as Vinny mimics old boxing moves to show a more masculine reaction to seeing his friend healthy.

"How do you feel, man? I thought we were going to lose you," says Vinny.

"I feel alive, I mean more alive than I have ever felt. Whatever they did, they did well," responds Ethan.

Vinny and Sophia begin looking him over with amazement as if he was reborn marveling at the rejuvenated presence that seems to glow from Ethan. After a few moments, Ethan gets tired of the gawking and childishly brushes them away. Vinny eager to show off the relics grabs Ethan by the shoulders and points at his early discoveries.

"Can you believe the history here? Hell they probably have Hoffa down here," says Vinny with a slight giggle.

"To be honest, Vinny, I played possum while in recovery, and they have a huge interest in us, but the two elders seemed to argue over our place here. They have been here a long time and want the world to know the truth, but they don't agree on our place and the approach to take," says Ethan.

The three of them stare at each other with confusion as if stumped by a challenging riddle before Sophia disrupts the silence.

"Maybe they want world peace and want to save the animals."

"Sophia, I'm sure they didn't travel through thousands of galaxies to become a SPCA member, staying hidden for thousands of years to help homeless cats in today's troubled times," jokes Ethan.

From the distance, you hear an uncomfortable chuckle as Amun and Yhovah enter the room.

"No, it isn't about the cats, but she isn't that far off. We are here exposed to save you, the human race, from extinction. Follow me," says Amun.

With yet another puzzled face shared among the friends, they follow the elders into a chamber. The room is dim and cool and has a musty smell; in the center is a grand pedestal with a large, thick book that's seems to demand Amun's respect. As the three stand patiently shrouded with mystery, they hear Yhovah say, "This begins your journey of understanding."

Chapter 16

B ack in Washington, the president and the admiral prepare to fly to the United Nations in New York where thousands wait to discuss or even debate about the phenomenon. The admiral gets on board the helicopter behind the president anxious to meet with leaders around the world hoping for a peaceful resolve.

"Terence, don't you think if they were hostile we would have been attacked already?" asks the admiral.

"I'm not sure, Daniel. They did attack a Russian vessel, and my fear is they are plotting their attack while we hope for peace. Some advisers believe their intent is hostile, and it would be in our best interest to be defensive and focus our resources on a weakness to a potential threat," responds the president.

"Weakness? To an alien race that lived on our planet for maybe thousands of years undetected with technology far more advanced than ours? I see no weakness, but I do see a shit load of fear," says the admiral.

"What makes you confident in the idea that they are not hostile? You said it yourself they attacked the Russian warship," asks the president.

"No, what I said was they disabled them with a procession attack. They never attacked to kill, and they attacked after they destroyed the civilian ship. They did it before the random gunfire from the Russian ship damaged anything else," says the admiral.

"I believe we still have to be prepared if they are hostile, but my gut says their intent is different. If there is any peaceful resolve, I want to find it," responds the president.

"Terence, as you can imagine, I have opened my mind a bit more to the concept of alien life. I spent time the last few days searching the Internet on alien theories. One particular theory seemed interesting. They call themselves ancient alien theorists or ancient astronauts," says the admiral.

"Ancient alien theorists? What is their theory? I will tell you this, I'm open to anything at this point, and if you're intrigued, then there must be some merit," responds the president.

"Well, their thought is that life here was begun by aliens. It suggests that thousands of years ago they helped develop and advance the evolution of modern man," answers the admiral.

"You sure this isn't some overactive imagination by some video game-hyped adolescent that dwells in fantasy worlds riddled with wizards and demons," giggles the president.

"I find that amusing, seeing how we fly low beneath an alien race that hovers in a grid pattern from our ocean floors! To answer your stupid question, no! These are in some cases very educated people who have PhDs and have done extensive work in archeology. There is evidence of sunken cities, the interpretations of ancient text, and the engineering of places like Gaza and the pyramids and the Mayans. The one thing I will say is this, add the word alien to any open question throughout histories' ancient past, and it becomes evident they could be a big part of the missing link," says the admiral.

"I don't know, Daniel. Why now? The theory seems to be an easy way to explain the unexplained. So assume the theory is correct, because it's all I have to go on, let's open the Internet and look into this deeper. I want to find the common denominator in all this," responds the president.

"Well historians are specific about the time line we all learned in grade school. However, there are many things that don't add up. I want to show you some of the most shared sights to see their perspective," says the admiral as he opens a laptop and begins to search the Internet.

"If you look at these pictures, you see ancient cave drawings of odd creatures or these statues of beings wearing what looks like a breathing apparatus. I would shrug most of this off if we were in a different situation, but based on the circumstances, how can we? Look at the Nazca lines, Egyptian megaliths that show precision cuts, the Indian Sanskrit and their heavy beliefs from 300 BC with details of flying machines called Vimanas. I also looked at other nationalities, American Indians believed in star people, the Chinese legend of Huangdi, and the global belief of the Sumerian tablets that detail the alien race of Anunnaki. It's not just ancient past. In 1974, there was the Betz Sphere and the wedge of Aiud that defied all sciences," points out the admiral.

"It appears they are believed to be responsible for plague and slavery, along with human crossbreeding, which means we could be a giant petri dish. The other thing is power. Imagine primitive man seeing flying crafts and odd-looking beings that have advanced science coming from the sky. They would see them as a higher power and treat them like gods. Not many people can handle power, Daniel, and they soon believe what others think of them. History also shows great conflicts and animosity whose core is from greedy kings and thickheaded religious beliefs. This ancient alien's theory seems possible, but I don't see it all sunshine and rainbows. I think there is a dark side," responds the president.

They continue to search through countless theories none more ridiculous than the other and try to prepare for what lies ahead at the United Nations.

Chapter 17

Amun and Yhovah appear to pray and make symbols in the air over the large book resting on the pedestal. There is a large high back chair with magnificent carvings in the wood that Yhovah sits in as Amun draws his attention to Sophia, Ethan, and Vinny.

"Today, my friends, is the beginning of a revelation. Mankind will know the truth of its purpose and origin. I need you three to help me share the message, because without you, this world is doomed to end. Much of what I will tell you may be hard to absorb. It may cause great conflict and anger inside you, and all I ask is you to maintain an open mind," starts Amun.

"At this point, my mind is wide open. Very little will surprise me," states Ethan with a slight smirk. Amun smiles back and begins opening the book. He slightly closes his eyes as if he fears the results of what needs to be said.

"We are known as Dogans. Our existence is but a whisper in your history, but we have been called many things. The most common has been a figment of your imagination, an urban legend, and/or government cover-ups. The truth is we have been here before your history even started. We have a great responsibility here, and that was to pass on the gift of intelligent life," says Amun.

"So you're saying you're responsible for the origin of man that what has been written in the Bible or science books are wrong?" says Vinny with some sense of aggression.

"Please, Vinny, keep an open mind, and understand what your soul already knows. You said it yourself—the world is not a prison house but a kind of spiritual kindergarten where millions of bewildered infants are trying to spell God with all the wrong blocks, a very accurate statement. The Bible you speak of is a written book with chapters by a series of people who described their primitive interpretations of things they didn't understand. The Bible tells tales from their views of teachings, our goals, and us. Understand that writing was new to them, life was as well, and much of what they wrote was a misinterpretation due to their primitive mind-set. God is taught that he is a spiritual being that created you, watched over you, and in the end will judge you. The truth is God is much larger than that, and the human brain can't handle that magnitude. What you need to understand is before that era, in a time when we came, the world was ravaged by large beasts and a slightly intelligent primate with immense amount of potential," continues Amun.

"So you came here when dinosaurs ruled and Neanderthal man was the closest thing to today's man, but the question is why here and why us?" asks Ethan.

"Patience, Ethan. Much will be revealed, but perhaps to understand, you have to know the meaning of life. You ask why, and it's simple, to exist. The gift of life started billions of years ago in origins way beyond here. Soon, the beginning of life became intelligent and spiritual. They developed into outer space, and it became clear that they needed to search for other intelligent life. They soon came upon a distant galaxy and planets with other primitive beings. They took a little of their own DNA and added it to help develop a better species and pass on their legacy. They watched as they developed into an intelligent entity that was eager to search beyond their galaxies, and so began the cycle of life and its meaning, to take a piece of your world and all that you are and pass it along with all before you and give purpose to the next entity that will carry the gift of life. This world and the primitive species that inhabited it were the next level of life, and we came to pass on that gift. In the beginning, we took some key elements of our DNA and added it to your Neanderthal man. Within a few generations, modern man took surface, and the once primate began to evolve into the type of entity called human beings. The human race now was the new vessel of millions of generations of life before it, but like a newborn, you needed to be nurtured," continues Amun.

Amun goes into detail of the process in how their DNA is meshed with human DNA and through an animated sequence on a visual hologram next to him shows the several stages of Neanderthal man to common man. Vinny seems uncomfortable with the idea of the Bible being wrong, while Ethan and Sophia seem to get intrigued.

"Man, this is like watching history channel but better," says Ethan.

"Ethan, you just were told all you know and believed in about life is a lie, and you're excited?" replies Vinny.

"Bro, I never believed in what was taught. I never could understand science and religion. They had way too many blank spots filled with the word faith. If the teachings of Adam and Eve as written in the Bible are fact, then why are there hundreds of other religions with their own idea? Then there is science. For several generations, science has the world believing that somewhere buried in sand or rock is the missing link. Well fuck religion and fuck science. The missing link is standing right in front of you," says Ethan in a defensive tone as he points to Amun.

"My friends, please don't argue. There is much more you need to know and understand, and both science and religion are correct. Let me explain," says Amun with a comforting grin and then continues. "Science is correct with early man, and religion is correct with about Adam and Eve, at least the idea of them. The primitive being that inhabited this planet were an advanced primate that walked upright, but they turned into modern man once our DNA was introduced. The first two humans that were created existed as one male and one female, and they were created in a lab. To teach man this story, we gave them names, within the story those names translated into Adam and Eve. The unforeseen issues followed after the development of Adam and Eve, creating the story of the forbidden fruit, which was symbolic of knowledge. The generation that followed began forming tribes and basic civilizations. We didn't anticipate the core of your own DNA that relied heavily on your primate instincts. As your species developed, it became evident that your strongest character trait was the alpha male syndrome. This was a natural survival characteristic throughout all mammals on this planet that insured stronger offspring and strength among leaders in packs or prides. The rules are to not interfere with the core characteristics of any developed species and expected this trait to become an asset not your demise."

Vinny and Ethan stare with confusion, and both say, "Demise?" as Sophia laughs.

"Yes!" responds Amun as he continues.

"Psychologically, it became evident that direction was needed along with purpose. Your minds were sponges sucking in vast amount of knowledge, what became evident were the inability to understand the wealth of information given. Your first civilization was uncontrollable, hostile, and destructive. We needed something for them to fear. We developed the concept of reward and discipline, not only immediate but also everlasting. We saw that by fearing discipline for negative actions kept the violence manageable, and on the opposite end, reward for the positive action only increased the results. Within a few generations, the stories became legend and detailed forming into many names, but you know them as heaven and hell. They feared permanent repercussions like the stories of hell, or the underworld, and Hades but strive for reward in places like heaven or places of divine nature surrounded by gods. We used this to maintain control and began forming a basic religion turning an unstructured beast into a fate-fearing intelligent life-form. This however had an unforeseen issue that turned man against himself and in many ways became your demise."

"So you are saying that there is no heaven or hell, that after you die you just become dust," interrupts Vinny.

"And why is that so difficult to believe? That seems easier than believing we float to some pearly gates and streets of gold or dropping into a lake of fire and suffering for eternity," shouts Ethan.

"I only ask you this. How would we know? Every being before you has theories of an afterlife, but only the dead can have the true answers. The larger issues were that of distinction, distinction of what was right or wrong, or what a god was or was not. Soon, the new mind of man turned to the beings that taught them. The concept of god wasn't enough or heaven or even hell for that matter. They soon turned to us as a divine entity, and we became the symbol of their newfound religion. Our crafts came from the sky, and this is the premise as to why heaven must be above you. Natural phenomenon became hell such as volcanoes and their destruction of fire that all shot from the center of Earth. This is why hell is below you. It was this belief that began an interesting direction into mainstream religion. Humans became obsessed with rewards and lost sight of their limits. They would stop at nothing to please us. At first, it was statues and minor monuments but soon turned into sacrifice and misguided violence. We lost control of what we started because the power of the alpha male needed to show us they were more dedicated than the others were. As the population grew, people took religion with them forming opinions and adding their own concepts and beliefs. Soon like a wildfire, man had expanded into a third of the world, and no two ideas of religion and us were the same, and it was again time for the alpha male to show itself. Religion became an idea that needed to be expressed, and each believed that their idea was the correct one. As this developed, so did animosity toward other people's opinions and interpretations, and soon violence and wars became in itself divine, for these wars were holy wars interpreted as justifiable and glorified. The most basic of concepts meant to manage a primitive species became misguided ideas that are still being fought today all over this beautiful planet, and to make it worse, this misguided idea has fueled wars for thousands of years. As the human race advanced, so did your wars, forcing you to rape your planet of its natural resources to feed that instinct of the alpha male and the glory of being told someday that your idea, your religion, or nation was the right one all along. The thought is to destroy anyone who opposes your beliefs and way of life, and in the end, the strongest faith wins. The sad truth is that when it is over and if someone can hold their crown up and declare themselves a winner, they will realize that they have won nothing but loneliness and disparity on a dying planet," explains Amun as he closes the book.

"This is a lot to absorb, and I want to you take what I have taught you and allow it to open your mind. The more you accept without prejudice, the more you will understand as this goes on.

Go and rest, and we will continue this soon. We have just begun to scratch the surface," finishes Amun and walks away.

Vinny abruptly begins heading back to the room with Ethan and Sophia in tow. The time of reflection and of the words heard will rip through Vinnie's head like a plague questioning everything he is and what he has done. Back in the room, it's only a matter of seconds before Ethan strikes up an argument by expressing his opinion.

Chapter 18

The president and the admiral aboard the helicopter continue scouting through Web pages trying to put pieces of the ancient alien theory together. The president who at first was very sarcastic seems to be intrigued by the level of proof many sites have presented.

"You know, Daniel, I find it odd that so much of this is shrugged off as ridiculous and misdirected theories. I guess one could say I'm bias now because of the alien presence has exposed itself, but much of this seems to need explanation. I would say our egos have blocked some sense of reason, but in some cases, the creditability of some individuals can't be questioned. You have engineers pointing out precision and mathematical calculations showing equal precision that cannot be answered, never mind the countless pilots and government agency members. To build the pyramids in ancient Egypt, those blocks would have had to been placed every three seconds to build them in twenty-two years. Each block weighed in at several tons being moved by hundreds of men with basic tools. We couldn't do it today with our current technologies and advanced understanding of physics and engineering. I would also ask why would you do something so difficult. Lord knows I wouldn't. They also lined them up perfectly facing true north, and it sits at the center of the landmass of the earth. The design has been seen all over the globe suggesting that the technology was shared even though they could never have interacted," points out the president.

"On that same idea, Terence, some theorist point out that people of great importance had similar attributes. Throughout the world, many cultures bound their children's head with rope to extend the skull's form and disfiguring them. The history of this says that it was done to honor the gods. Of the pharaohs in ancient Egypt, all the hieroglyphics showed elongated baldheads, again to honor the gods or to symbolize their belief that they themselves where gods. I would agree that much of this seems hindsight due to our current situation, but it also seems ridiculous that it went ignored or revered as unimportant," responds the admiral.

The flight is a little turbulent, but the admiral and the president seem not to notice. As they enter into the New York City airspace, a shimmer of light catches the president's eye directing his attention outside the window.

"Lieutenant, are we in the metropolitan area?" asks the president.

"Yes, sir, the decoys flew by way of the coastline, but we came in from inland. We are just entering the Bronx and over the George Washington Bridge. It's nice not to pay the tolls," jokes the pilot.

"You know, Daniel, this is a beautiful city. I grew up forty-five minutes away. I remember weekend trips to the ballpark, Time Square, and shopping on Fordham Rd for school clothes. I miss those simple times when I could look at this city and marvel at its beauty," says the president.

"I believe you still see it. I know I do. I miss all my youth in this city, from soccer and little league to GI Joes and skateboarding. I think a lot about my adult life and the bases of my motivation to join the Navy. In the end, it was to preserve the right to be a kid, those years of comfort that this nation gave me to enjoy being a child. I believe that every child should enjoy the simplicity of life that comes with childhood, to wake up and go outside and play, or take a trip to a ballpark and not worry about a nation's war or political and religious beliefs interfering with my innocence," says the admiral.

"That's not the case today. The city is ravaged with poverty and economic turmoil like most of our nation. Now this event could take an injured nation and bring it to our knees. I question the timing and the ideas of coincidence. I'm a firm believer that most things are not done by accident," responds the president.

"Or it could bring this nation together as a unified front, bringing back the pride that we had when we said we were Americans.

Remember 9/11? There is nothing stronger than unified nation, Terence. Nothing!" answers back the admiral.

The president grins and lets out a small humored exhale as if inspired by their simple thoughts of their cherished childhoods. The skyline of the once proud city engulfs the helicopter as it begins to land by the UN building. They are greeted by a small army of heavily armed soldiers eager to get the president inside. The slight hums of the alien crafts still in the grid pattern tighten the air reminding the president that the memories of his childhood were just that—memories.

Chapter 19

The walk back from the chamber seemed endless as Ethan becomes relentless in getting into Vinnie's head. Sophia, feeling uncomfortable, trails behind them avoiding any opportunity of confrontation allowing them the room they need to vent.

"Don't just keep walking, bro. Answer me. Why is this so hard for you to comprehend?" shouts Ethan as he scratches his right hand.

They enter the room that they have been resting in, and Vinny walks right to the ancient relics that litter the area. The musty smell and history-soaked objects seem to comfort his unsettled mind as he stares aimlessly at everything in the room. Ethan frustrated by the one-sided debate throws his feet up on a table and eats some plums and grapes from a wooden bowl. Vinny walks deeper into the artifacts surrounding himself with his beliefs and doubts as Sophia follows to offer support.

"There is more to this, Vinny. What's on your mind? I'm here to listen," says Sophia.

Vinny holding back some emotion looks at Sophia and throws his hands up as if confused.

"More? More than this, this shit! Life wasn't easy for me, Sophia, and at times the only thing I had was faith. Now all those times I sat alone crying and begging for help were empty and meaningless. I'm being told no one heard me or cared, and my faith in something larger than what I can understand and it was actually an ugly gray old man living miles below me in the ocean," shouts Vinny.

Sophia can't help but laugh at his serious but yet comedic description of Amun, but she realizes there is more going on in Vinnie's mind.

"I understand the magnitude of the impact this must have on you, Vinny, but it seems to have a deep-rooted meaning for you that you're holding back on. Let it out," asks Sophia.

Vinny turns to Sophia with his eyes slightly watered and crouch to the floor looking tired and distraught.

"My life was confusing. I felt abandoned at times. When I looked around for a father's advice and no one was there. My mother is a wonderful person. Many times she played the father role with me by playing catch outside or letting me practice wrestling moves on her, but as I got older, I needed more. I needed a male role model to explain all the crazy things going on in my head, and when I couldn't get the answers, I turned to my faith to ease the frustrations. I found comfort in my beliefs and what they stood for. I believed something much larger than me was watching me, loving me, and caring for me from heaven. I believed that my emptiness would be filled by rewards of eternal life surrounded by roads paved in gold. Today, I learned that those memories, emotions, and beliefs are false, and the joy I had in knowing something great was waiting for me were misguided. I believe the very foundation of who I am is based on those memories, and my life was built on that understanding. Now I feel like the one strength I had has been destroyed, and my very character now stands weak and vulnerable. Today, I'm told that in those future moments when I feel alone and I pray to God for comfort, no one is listening," says Vinny, as he lowers his head to hide his tears.

"Vinny, I don't think you listened when Amun was speaking. He said that God is larger than that. He said we couldn't conceive the true nature of what God is. Life has its hard times and challenging moments for all of us. I believe how we overcome them is what determines our paths in life. You cry because you didn't have a father, and when life had some turmoil, you felt alone. You found comfort in your faith, and it's what gave you strength. You can call it God or faith, you can call it alcohol or drugs, and you can call it sports or work. In the end, it's what allowed you to make it through the bullshit. I don't talk much to many people about my childhood, but I will say I envy you. I thought I had a wonderful family, a loving family. We were so close, and many of us shared a home together where generations shared dinner tables every night. As I got older, I realized I was a lucky girl. Many of my friend's parents were divorced. Many of them didn't know their uncles or aunts, grandparents or cousins, even fathers or mothers, and I felt sad for them. In my early teens, I remember a Friday night. It was a full moon, and the moonlight lit up my room like daytime. My window was on a crack, so I smelled some fresh-cut spring grass and crisp linen sheets, my very definition of serenity. I heard my door squeak open and looked to see if my cousin Christopher had come in to sleep next to me after a scary movie like usual. In the doorway, I saw a silhouette of a familiar person as it walked to the foot of my bed. As the person cleared the shadows and entered the moonlight, I saw it was my dad. He was crying and distraught. I was hurt to see him upset and begged him to tell me what was wrong. He sat on the side of my bed and leaned kind of close and just said, "I'm sorry." I quickly noticed the smell of the linen sheets and cut grass were dwarfed by cheap whiskey and became concerned. He stood up, turned his back to me, and before I could get a word out, he turned and backhanded me across the face. I was dazed and couldn't seem to focus, and before I passed out, all I saw was him undoing his belt. In the morning, I woke up with a crisp sun in my face and a morning breeze, but not the clean sheets. Between my legs was a small amount of pooled blood, and my body began to ache. I was so confused and just started to cry violently screaming for my mother or someone in the house. I ran down the hall and burst through my parent's bedroom door looking for comfort. The moment I entered the room, my nightmare became worse. My father's rage had unleashed, and after taking my innocence, he killed my mother and then himself. I ran out the door and into the Nevada desert. With no purpose or direction, I just ran. I found myself among mountains and sand and alone, and I just fell face down, and when I woke up, six months had passed, and I was surrounded by strangers that pitied me, and doctors and detectives that wanted to talk about my relationship with my family. There was nothing to talk about. Up to that moment, I felt like I had a perfect family life. I ran away from there and lived in several foster homes over the years, but I found my comfort in supporting other victims or potential victims and protesting against the monsters that took my life away. God to me was watching a little girl saved from experiencing what I lived through because I helped. You cry because you had no father, but I envy you because you didn't have mine, and I'm sure my story wouldn't hold a candle to other peoples throughout this world. I believe life has meaning even when life is fucked up, and if you're strong enough to live through all the bullshit, then your reward is the experience of life," says Sophia, as she does her best to hide an exposed tear.

Vinny feels compelled to comfort Sophia somehow but remains distant feeling like he has no right. Sophia leans against the wall next to Vinny and tosses his right arm up and snuggles into the curve of his neck and plays with the hairs on his other arm. Vinny embraces Sophia gently and gives a soft kiss to the top of her head letting her know he had no right to complain.

"So what about your brother?" asks Sophia.

"He really isn't my brother. He was my childhood best friend. In ninth grade, we decided we were brothers, and no one will tell us different. From that day on we had each other's back, and we vowed never to break our bond. As we got older, I wanted to go to school, and he wanted to see the world, but we never lost touch. This is the longest we have been apart without any communication, and I feel empty, but I'm glad you're here," says Vinny.

The two stand up and sit by the table that Ethan had commandeered knowing the debate was about to open.

"So you gonna talk to me or what?" shouts Ethan.

Sharing a smirk with Sophia, Vinny leans over the table and prepares to engage in the battle.

"Ethan, I understand your vision. I really do. I guess my biggest debate is why now. I understand the disaster may be the springboard, but I feel there is more to this than just peace and harmony."

"You just can't let go of the misguided beliefs you had. The truth is in your face, and you refuse to acknowledge it. All my life the theory of God and the devil or heaven and hell confused me. If there is a god, why is there disease or war? Why is there divorce and rape? Something as magnificent as God should be able to wipe that away in a moment. I watched countless television shows of people's translations of how they saw God and why this world is as fucked up as it is, and they had the answer if you were willing to pay twenty dollars to find out in their new book. Religion is a business that lives off the weak, and while the world starves, it keeps getting fat. Reality is flesh and blood even if it's an alien because I can see it and hear it, not a fairy tale written thousands of years ago," says Ethan as he continues to scratch his right hand.

"What's wrong with your hand? Why are you scratching it?" asks Sophia.

"Let me see it," says Vinny.

Reluctantly, Ethan leans his hand over the table exposing a slight blue round mark just under his skin. Vinny being intrigued jumps over to another table grabbing what looks like a magnifying glass and hovers it over Ethan's hand.

"Dude, it's a pulsing light and symbol. When the light flashes, you see an actual pattern. I have seen the pattern before on some of the ancient hieroglyphs here in this room. I would say it's their stamp or signature," points out Vinny.

"It's the size of pencil's eraser. Let me see the magnifying glass," asks Sophia.

The two continue to gawk at the faded light and pattern and describe the image that appears as it pulses.

"It looks like three sperm heads with curled tails or three nines," says Sophia.

"It could be sixes, Sophia. Three sixes and you know what that means?" says Vinny as he seems to indulge in deep thought about his newfound revelation.

"What the hell was that about? I think he is losing his freaking mind, Sophia. I mean he is out there with all this shit," says Ethan.

"I can't say I know what he thinks a lot of the times, but I can say that his motivation is to have our best intentions in mind," answers Sophia.

The three start to feel the effects of their overworked and now exhausted mind. Vinny continues to wonder the relics as Sophia curls up in a ball on the oversized bed. Ethan still a bit flustered and aggravated leans against the wall in a chair by the table and begins to dose as he finds the position quite comfortable. Vinny looks at his friends and just embraces the thought that he isn't facing this alone. He quietly throws a blanket on Ethan and then curls up around Sophia absorbing her warmth and compassion with each breath she takes. He begins to feel like what ever gets thrown his way he can handle it with her by his side. As he dwells in the comfort, he closes his eyes and prepares himself for whatever life may throw his way tomorrow.

Chapter 20

The flags crack as the winter air rushes around the UN court-yard. The soldiers pressed close to the admiral and the pres-ident giving little room of deviation from the path they set as they head to the front gate. Their weapons are pointed up as they anticipate any attack coming from the alien grid above forming a cocoon made of cautious and alert rifles. The president feeling con-fined presses toward the front door eager to avoid the uncomfortable vibe from the overanxious young soldiers.

"At ease, soldiers. I think we are safe now," states the president.

"Sir! Yes, sir!" shouts the energetic Marine.

The two enter the grand entrance, and both seem to absorb the genuine experience the UN brings when you enter it. Every home-land security branch special agent dedicated to getting them into the central conference center surrounds them, where hundreds of world leaders have joined anticipating some direction.

"Do you remember being that energetic that disciplined and gung ho when we were that young?" asks the admiral.

"I think our duty remains the same and discipline, but I believe our experience and age has toned down our energy a bit. It's not like we are twenty something and jumping off battleship decks into pending doom with no regard for our safety like we used to," says the president as he taps the bandages on the admiral's arm, slightly mocking his heroics.

"President or not, You can kiss my ass, Terence," snaps the admiral as they enter the large general assembly area.

Several associates who are dedicated in maintaining an edu-cated opinion in the proper way to address the UN meet them front and center again. The president smiles to embrace their support and council by nodding his head but pushes through them as he carries the opinion of his best friend with him to be himself. He stands at the front of the room and absorbs the glare of everyone's patience and anticipation of what he has to say. He takes in this moment because this is the pride of what America once stood for; the world depended on the ideas and support of this strong nation. The day he took office, he knew his battle would be to regain the respect of the nations that saw America as a failed idea and supported or feared the politics of the new superpower in Russia. This moment was his chance to shine, to prove to the world we are here to support a unified front, and America is as it always was a backbone of diplomacy. He takes a deep breath and taps the microphone to be sure his words are heard; and without any fear of regret, he lets what's on his mind expose itself to the intrigued room.

"My friends, we have been through some troubled times over the years. I don't speak as a man swollen with experiences here, but as a nation scared by generations of misguided prejudices. Today, more than ever, we need to realize we need to put aside our petty differences and focus more on our common grounds. We need to look in the mirror and see ourselves not as Americans, Russians, or any other nationality but as human beings. We take for granted that though many of us are thousands of miles apart, this is only inches in the grand scheme of things. A few days ago, chaos struck our world as oil threatened the entire ecosystem of the Atlantic Ocean. Moments later, we are saved by an intelligent life force that may have been sharing our world for thousands of years. We as human beings watched as our skies became filled with foreign entities, and we allowed fear to consume our conscious and rational thought. We as human beings challenged the idea that anything not human must be inferior, and we took it upon ourselves to make the decision for an entire race to deem it hostile. We once again allowed our prejudices to shine and control our better judgment and attacked something we didn't understand. There was only one problem. We didn't provoke or intimidate them. We didn't force them to lower their standards and attack us. Even now among our ignorance, they hover above us without hostile intent or aggression. They came from our waters, and as most of you sit here comfortable with our armies or bodyguards, the east river sits only a few yards away possibly filled with alien life ready to communicate or even attack. My opinion is that for once, we need to join as a race not separate nations to offer a solution and method to this risk or reward. I have no direct answer to the action we need to take, but I am confident in the maturity of this group that as a majority we will agree in the direction going forward."

The crowd cheers to the comfort of his idea, but as he looks around the room, not everyone seems to be in agreement with him. He notices that the lead to the disagreement falls on the Russian prime minister as he raises his hands to silence the crowd.

"My friends, how can we listen to a president that may very well be to blame for this accident and feeds the continued downward spiral of a once powerful and proud nation?" says the prime minister.

"How do we know these crafts aren't an advanced technology of the US government taking the opportunity of a possible disaster to invade our air space and privacy? We watched the news and saw what television broadcasted, but we have no proof this wasn't just a ploy to launch this invasion of our borders," shouts a Middle Eastern delegate.

The room seems to part with opinions and talks of conspiracy; the moment of truth arises for the president to take his stand as a voice of reason extinguishing any doubt.

"My friends, we are experienced enough to know the expense of a mass deployment of this many crafts would be astronomical and far beyond our budget would allow. Our friends in Russia would have you believe this accident was a US issue, but the facts are clear. Both the vessels that where involved has specific origins. One was ported out of Portland, Maine, and owned by a private US company. The other was directly from Russia, and the accident was based on the two vessels refusing to share the international drilling station forcing unsafe docking procedures. The moment the storm hit, both guilty parties' incompetence allowed the ships to collide and forced them into the station rupturing two of the three main lines. To add to this chaos, both ships received damage to their hulls that lead to more oil spilling into the Atlantic. You speak of a powerful nation, Prime

Minister, and all I remember is a proud one. We went to the site with the intention to rescue and contain the obvious concerns, and we were welcomed by a combat fleet armed and ready to protect and hide the Russian involvement. Your government fired on the ships and did zero damage to these craft but did manage to destroy a US volunteer ship loaded with US civilians there to help assist in a rescue. As I speak to everyone in this room, you're being passed a copy of the manifest that gives you the names of each volunteer aboard this boat. Ladies and gentleman, it needs to be clear that of the sixty names on that list, we are sad to report we have no survivors. Yet I don't come here pointing fingers and demanding apologies because I am aware of the concerns and fears we all share. I refuse to question the judgment of a nation without having the opportunity to have seen it from their vantage point. What we did see was as the ship of volunteers splintered into millions of pieces from stray ammunitions, and these crafts defended themselves by attacking the most aggressive battleship. The question I have is, as I put this attack on the screen, I ask the Prime Minister how many lives were lost (interrupting his response). Sir, I believe that answer to be none! No nation in this room has the technology even in prototype to produce this firepower or precision (continuing to play a recorded video from a US ship), and no pilot could handle the forces generated by these maneuvers. Today, my friend, is the time to put aside this bullshit and focus not on the matters of blame or conspiracy but on unity and understanding. We just have been shown that we are not alone and that the gift of life on this planet is shared, and now we must concede the idea that we may not even be the most advanced species on this planet and for sure in this universe. Today, we need to realize we are one species and not many, and as one, we need to be prepared to welcome or defend our world as a place inhabited by a foreign entity. If nothing else is clear, please understands this. No one nation can deal with this alone, and without each other's support, we will fail. This entity has us outpopulated by an estimated twenty to one now with new data. It is now believed to be closer to one hundred to one globally."

The president continues to share his intelligence to all interested, but the admiral can't help to see a small group form around the

Russian prime minister. The admiral gets a gut feeling like something isn't right and casually tries to determine if his instincts are accurate.

Politics was never his forte, but he begins to mingle among the other brass to allow him the opportunity to hear what the rebel group is discussing. His attention is redirected as another admiral from the UK grabs his elbow and expresses similar concerns about the small group around the Russians.

"What do you think, admiral? No one in that party seems interested in a peaceful solution. Some people are only content when they are in control, and those people will have control any way they can."

"I don't feel right about this, admiral. Lewis and I may need the UK's support in the event this gets ugly. When I was in the Atlantic, I saw the strength of the Russian fleet. It was only dwarfed by the sheer power briefly displayed by our visitors. If I know the Russians, they're going to somehow get that power in their corner, by any means necessary."

He looks to see where Terence is but turns to see that the prime minister has separated himself from the crowd, as he tends to cell phone call. The Russian prime minister walks into a closed hallway to avoid being overheard, and this seems like the chance for the admiral to get some dirt on maybe where the Russians' mind-set is. He shakes a few hands and casually makes his way toward the hallway with all intentions of having some questions answered one way or the other.

Chapter 21

The night is unsettling, and the restless Vinny can't seem to sleep more than an hour at a time. He looks at Sophia and recognizes that his constant shifting is interrupting her sleep and slips off the bed to avoid waking her. Sophia still remains in a spooned position as Vinny circles around the bed facing her comforting face. He finds himself consumed by butterflies as her innocence warms his soul; somehow in all this, Vinny finds himself falling for Sophia, and he is okay with it.

"She is beautiful, bro, and I know you long enough to know when you are falling for someone."

Vinny turns to see Ethan looking over his shoulder and noticing the obvious attraction for Sophia.

"You know, Ethan, I have been with a few women in my time, but it has always been physical. I never looked into someone's true being and soul and became attracted to who they are. She has such compassion and dedication to what she believes in, and she will give 110 percent to protect it. She confided in me some personal things, and it made me realize that life is about moments not empty memories. I don't think I have ever had a zest for life like she has and such desire to help people and make a genuine difference. Then I think of these beings that say we were chosen to take on the wonderful gift of life to the next level. I can't help but remember sitting in our living room bitching about the entire negative shit on TV and the sick and cruel things humans do, and I ask do we deserve it. Does a race who murder and rape children, beat and abuse women, build weapons of mass destruction, and ravage a planet to a point of global warming deserve such a gift. We will take a little bit of this beast within us and pass it on to all future entities worthy of this gift tainting the perhaps millions before us and set them up for failure and self-destruction. The part that gets me is moments like this when I look at this beautiful young woman with such life. That I say yes, we have a gift to give, and I never knew it until a few days ago."

"When did you become all sappy and poetic? You are gonna make me throw up man!" smiles Ethan.

"Kiss my ass, Ethan," giggles Vinny as he walks toward the back area of the relics.

The rear of the large room has a translucent wall overlooking the ocean landscape and the wonderful city they are consumed by. The ocean floor has a deep purple hint and small splits in the seabed glow vibrant oranges and pinks from the molten rock below the surface. Small pockets of heated gas bubble from cooled mounds of lava push through the cracks. Fish of rare design seem to play among the bubbles, and they seem to absorb some of the ambient light around them as many show hints of pink and purple.

"I don't think Disney could picture something this pretty," says Ethan "You know, since we are being up front and personal, I want you to know something about me that no one knows," continues Ethan.

"Please don't tell me you like my ass or something, cause I can tell you it would put me over the edge," jokes Vinny.

"No you have a flat ass (giggling), but on a serious note, I have some demons. I was seventeen, and I had to be popular. I had to surround myself with all the cool kids and subject myself to the things they did to remain in the circle. My life was consumed by casual drugs, late-night beer runs, and endless drama about who was sleeping with whom. I remember a summer Friday night and being drunk off my ass and a girl I was into wanting to take me home. She had a nice Mustang with sexy rims and a stereo that could stop your heart. Anyway, she insisted I drive cause she was in worse shape than me. Maybe this was her way of getting me to go home with her, but man this car moved, and it was tight, and it had a deep roar when you touched the gas. I remember hitting this turn and the rear end breaking loose like out of the movies, and like a stunt car driver, I drifted that turn with smoke in my rearview mirror and the tires making a high-pitched melody. As soon as I cleared the turn, I hit the straightaway, and I realized I was on the wrong side of the road and then a heard a huge bang. I woke up and saw blood and wrecked metal everywhere and two people on the street. I must have hit this car head-on at eighty miles an hour, and I got tossed like forty feet and into the bushes. The girl I was with was dead, and all I saw was a car seat in the road by the other people. I had a scratch on my arm. That's it, a fucking miracle. But it soon became clear I was in for some serious shit, so I bailed. The next morning, the news reported that a female drunk driver crossed the double yellow line and killed herself and a family of three. I was free and clear, but her legacy was tarnished, and the cars filled with innocent people were dead, but I was fine. So maybe I never raped a child or abused a woman and I recycle, but I'm a monster still the same, and maybe I'm hoping all this chaos and talk of change will hide my guilt and depression that I'm forced to disguise every day. So maybe your dad was a prick and maybe Sophia had some issues in life, but I am sure neither of you killed four people and destroyed someone's reputation forcing you to stare at a villain, a monster, or a poor excuse of a human being at every reflection. If there is a God, then why would he allow me to get behind the wheel of that car? Why would he allow me to destroy four peoples' lives? If there is a God, he is horrible at his job, not just because of me but also because of you and anyone else who has been tormented by what life dealt them. It is easier for me to believe in a living being and DNA transfers that made some mistakes. It's easier for me to blame them than to accept that God has a reason for why shit happens, and I have to have faith. I resent the idea that there is any reason in the world why God needed my drunk ass to kill anyone without retribution, and I resent the idea that faith is the answer."

Vinny is floored by the testimony Ethan reveals and sits speechless as Ethan walks away and sits in the chair wrapping himself up in a blanket. The story from Ethan only continues to fuel the frustration Vinny has toward the history and judgment of mankind. He begins to move toward the bed where Sophia is sleeping hoping that her innocence will comfort his discontent but notices a book on the table. It is thick and leather bound with some gold accents on the words "Holy Bible." It's older like all the relics maybe several hundred years old, and its writing is slightly faded, but Vinny feels compelled to read it. He feels comfort as he did in his childhood by looking toward his faith for guidance and deliverance even if something is telling him otherwise. He opens the cherished book and begins to read the faded text saying out loud, "I love the book of Revelation."

Chapter 22

The hallway echoes of the prime minister's shoes as he creates distance from anyone who might overhear his conversation. The loud noise from his shoes allows the admiral to sneak in and find an open room along the hallway so he can listen in on the conversation.

"We need to get control of this technology and use it to our advantage. The world is ripe for the picking, and with either the technology or the visitors on our side, no one can stand up to our power."

The admiral takes out his cell phone and dials the president's personal cell phone then places it on the floor, hidden in the doorway. He sneaks out the main assembly rushing toward the president. The admiral grabs the president and asks him for his cell phone so he would not lose connection.

"I can hear him perfectly. The echo in the room carries every word," says the admiral.

The admiral pulls the president to the side and hits the speakerphone as the two listen in on the conversation eager to hear where the Russians stand on the pending issue. Only seconds into the conversation does it become clear not all parties are on the same page.

"I do believe this moment is our opportunity to gain full control of America and its supporters. They are weak and depleted and would barely be able to survive an attack with our forces now. Add these visitors and/or their technology to the equation, and they would fall. We need a discreet means into getting the visitor's attention so we could partner with them or harness their technology. Either way, we do not have much time," says the prime minister.

After a few more quick statements, the prime minister makes his way to the main assembly room to rejoin his peers.

"I apologize. My wife called and just wanted to make sure I was okay," says the prime minister.

He appears to continue his conversation with others in his group as if the phone call was nothing, and the admiral couldn't be angrier.

"This is bullshit. I just listened as the prime minister discussed their hostile intent. Let me just shoot him," aggressively whispers the admiral to the president.

"That's not an option, Daniel. I do however want to have several black op teams watch the Atlantic fleet and report on any attempt to gain control of the visitors."

The admiral still angered makes his way to the same hallway and sarcastically excuses himself.

"It must be contagious. Now my wife is calling me. Please excuse me."

The admiral picks up his phone off the floor and makes several phone calls setting in motion two seal teams into the Atlantic who prepare to shadow the Russian fleet.

Back in the main assembly hall, several members around the Russian prime minister become restless and make a press toward progress.

"We appreciate that the US is scared of defending themselves and due to economic concerns need the members of this room to support their procrastination. However, we need to be aggressive in knowing these visitor's weaknesses and prepare for what could be a hostile intent," shouts an assembly member supporting the conversation around the Russian prime minister.

"I assure you the United States government is not procrastinating, but we do air on the side of caution. I refuse to jeopardize the safety of the American public and our allies in an attempt to agitate a possible advanced species. I refuse to stand by and watch a few people's ignorance separate any option of a peaceful resolve. You speak of procrastination, well let me say this. If any government takes it upon themselves to make a decision affecting the safety of America or any of its allies, I will see it as an act of war. The options are clear, ladies and gentleman. As a group, we will make a decision on our approach to this matter, and in the event someone stands alone and avoids a unified front, we will deem them hostile. At that moment, I will not procrastinate in attacking anyone who endangers the American people or a unified front. I know that the world may not see us as the powerful nation of the past, but the pride of the army is unmatched, and the power of self-preservation will make us a formidable foe. This is your moment, gentleman. Sit with us and trust in the people within this room, or challenge the fact that I'm prepared to kick your ass," boldly says the president.

The room becomes silent as the aggressive tone echoes throughout the grand assembly. Several members smirk as others begin to clap in support. Soon, the room is deafened by hundreds of nations prepared to stand behind the United States. The admiral smiles as he absorbs the unity and stands proud behind the aggressive approach of his friend and his president. The president looks to his friend and says, "Man, I went all in on that one. I almost shit my pants. Maybe next time, I should prepare a speech."

The admiral laughs and walks into the supportive crowd taking a seat next to some of his associates who now wait to hear the next step. The crowd settles, and several members start to issue their opinions on the next steps.

"I believe a broadcast in several languages from this building should be sent alerting the entities of our peaceful intent. I also believe that the center of diplomacy should be recognized as this building, and in the broadcast, we should make it clear that we expect any communication to be done through the center," states the English prime minister.

"I support that decision, but I believe we need to consider simple methods as well such as Morse code or other basic means of communications with a time limit, maybe a signal that slowly fades representing a countdown," says the Italian prime minister.

"How about smoke signals or arrows drawn in the sand?" says the Russian prime minister sarcastically.

"I don't appreciate your sarcasm, Prime Minister, but what I believe we can do is broadcast a looping signal that fades each time filtered into a forty-eight-hour window and block all other signals forcing the signal and direction here," states the president.

Several members begin to nod showing signs of agreement, but the Russian prime minister seems discontent. He begins walking again toward the hallway and begins dialing on his cell phone. As the rest of the room begins to discuss the next steps of the contents of the message, the admiral makes his way toward the Russian prime minister. The prime minister is several rows in front of the admiral and makes his way into the hallway quickly.

"This is not going as planned. The Americans have managed to gain support. We need to be aggressive. The plan is to get the alien's attention and get them on board with us. Let them know we are the dominant race, and force them to assist us in getting control. Our focus is to portray the Americans as gun-slinging cowboys that need to be put under control. We need to broadcast whatever images we can of the aggressive US. I'm talking Vietnam and the atom bomb, anything that makes them hostile looking, and if the aliens don't comply, then we need to harness their technology. Make it happen, General," says the prime minister.

As he closes his phone, he hears his voice echo in the general assembly area and sees the admiral at the end of the hallway with his phone in hand.

"I had my phone on speaker, Prime Minister, and I called the president who also had his phone on speaker. The president moved his phone close to the podium microphone to share your discussion with the entire room. Your intentions are known and your plans a bust," shouts the admiral.

The prime minister looks around for a quick exit but soon realizes he is trapped in the hall.

"I have diplomatic—"

But before he can finish his sentence, he is thrown to the floor violently by the admiral and knocked unconscious. Several military police surround the prime minister and his supporters who pick him up and contain them all. The prime minister tries to find his footing as he recovers from the admiral's blow. A man gives the prime minister a handkerchief to wipe the blood from his face and mouth, but he refuses it and shouts, "It doesn't matter. The order has been given. I challenge your threat, Mr. President, and declare war on America and its allies. We will win this by any means necessary, and these aliens will join us or die."

Chapter 23

The comforting glow of the ocean floor and its elegant harmony seems to hypnotize Vinny. The soft blues and faint pastels accent the room, and Vinny looks behind him, as Sophia seems at peace in her sleep. Ethan seems to have a relaxed face as if talking to Vinny may have relieved some of the demons he carried over the years. Vinny however seems more lost than ever with such conflict over his beliefs and the new facts before him. He soon hears a light shuffle and turns to see Amun approaching him.

"You seem so conflicted, Vinny. You're different than most, and I think you deserve to know more. Follow me," says Amun.

"Our history isn't too far from yours, Vinny. Our world was colder consumed by water. We had a very hard time with the gift given to us, and our world was heavily divided. We had a natural disaster that threatened the entire water system or basically our way of life. It was then that our gift givers were introduced, the Anunnaki. It took years for us to change and come together as a dying world and develop into future gift givers ourselves," states Amun.

"Why us? It wouldn't appear we had anything to give," says Vinny.

"You don't realize that the human race has beautiful traits and is nowhere near their true potential. To be funny, my primitive ancestors were nothing more than a smart fish (chuckling). We had to get beyond our egos and realize that we would fail to exist if we didn't come together, and we did," stresses Amun.

"How do we convince this world to come together. World peace has become an urban legend as much as you have," says Vinny.

"Evidence. It's all around this wonderful world. Our intervention litters this planet, and it's the human ego that blinds the obvious. Technology has made this more evident with the Internet and developing science. Hundreds of years ago, the world was flat, and the Earth was the center of the galaxy. A hundred years ago, the concept of distant galaxies and other planets was folklore and harsh theories, but today, it's fact that there are billions of planets and that the Earth is round and that you're not the center of the galaxy. Places like Egypt and their Pyramids or the Mayans and their technology scratch the surface. Places like Puma Punku, Lake Titicaca lost city, and Tiwanaku in Bolivia show our existence. We will present such compelling evidence that all the world's leaders will have to listen and heed our warning. Vinny, the time has come to judge. This world has failed four times already, and we were forced to destroy more than 90 percent of mankind each time. The time has come again to decide if this level of man is capable of progress and developing into the entity that we need to further the cycle of life. We as Asuras do not have much time left, and without us, the cycle of life may very well end here, and billions of evolved generations from equal amount of galaxies will die with you. Your DNA has millions of alien species coded into you, and your failure destroys them and the future of their legacy being passed. We refuse to let that happen," says Amun as he rests his rugged hand on Vinnie's shoulder.

Off to the right, Yhovah walks in with a small devise. It looks a lot like a pistol with thin needle for a barrel, and it glows from the center with a teal tone.

"What the hell is that?" asks Vinny.

"Salvation!" replies Yhovah.

"This is a micro-beacon that will be inserted into your hand. It's DNA coded, and if we determine the destruction of man is needed only 144,000, specific humans will be saved based on the genetic code they display. This insertion of the beacon means you're among the gifted and chosen to inherit the Earth and progress the gift of life. To refuse this is suicide. Unfortunately, if the time comes to filter this planet, only the chosen will survive. That I promise you," says Amun.

"What about Sophia?" asks Vinny.

"She doesn't share the DNA signature that would allow her to inherit this planet," says Yhovah.

"Yhovah, have some compassion!" shouts Amun.

"What do you mean? She is the most pure person I have met," shouts Vinny, as his eyes seem to water.

"I understand your feelings, Vinny, but if we allow one that doesn't have the DNA code we need, then the future of the race is tainted and is doomed to fail. This isn't an option. It's a choice but one only you can make. We will leave you be to decide, but tomorrow, we need to address the world's leaders. You have till then," says Amun.

The two walk away into the now dreary glow of the room, and Vinny sees nothing but despair and discontent. He has fallen in love and now is forced to turn his back on it or die for it, and the chaos that is has become almost more than he can bear. With tears running down his face, he once again finds comfort in the only book that has ever given him direction, the *Bible*.

Chapter 24

T he room has a heavy and awkward feel as the Russian prime minister is escorted to a holding area down the stairs. The president now has a genuine threat on his hands, and his actions can be crucial to the future of his nation.

"We must alert the entire defense network, Terence," says the admiral.

"I understand your concern, Daniel, but it's delicate. If we become overaggressive, then the Russians may gain instant support from some neutral groups. I also have to consider the idea that they have already begun to communicate with the visitors and campaign for their support. If that is the case, our aggressive approach may in fact force the visitors against us, and I assure you, we are no match for the technology they have displayed," replies the president.

"I assure you, every minute wasted is crucial, and if we don't show a little muscle, then those same neutral groups may see us as weak and support the Russians. This is our time to establish our place as the proud and strong nation we have always been. Each minute discussing this weakens the links that bind our allies and give strength to the hostile ideas of an already-aggressive adversary," states the admiral.

The pause seems endless as the president aggressively rubs his eyes and slowly drags his hands to cover his lips. He signals to the admiral and turns his back to the crowd. He whispers intently to the admiral and taps the podium assertively seeming to emphasize his orders and point. The admiral nods his head in understanding and quickly begins dialing from a phone walking away to assure his privacy. The room seems eager to know the direction of the United States and perhaps the side they choose to follow. The admiral comes rushing to the president's side as he approaches the podium. The two exchange quiet words, and the president grips his shoulder to express his content and taps the microphone as he prepares to address the room.

"Ladies and gentleman, make no mistake about it, we are at war. The question we ask now is who are we at war with? This is the moment we decide to stand in unity with morality and hold in regard the best interest of humanity and defend it. Or do we side with greed and deception whose ugly face only shows the disgusting glare of shallow power and domination? Domination of you and all you believe, the stripping of your right to decide. If the Russians win the power of this entity, we will stand up to a villain never seen before in this world. To stand up to this tyrant shows we believe in who we are, not as Americans or Europeans or any other great nation standing here but as humans who believe in the very core of what we are. This is the tale of David and Goliath, good versus evil, and in the end life over death. Today, you choose the side that the world will remember you by forever, not your past but what you chose for all of humanities' future. We have confirmation that twenty of the Russian's Atlantic fleet have met in force to turn the entities' power in to an ally or to harness it and use it. If we are to stop them, it needs to be now. If nothing else, it will be my dying breath that leads us to victory and the spirit of the people we defend."

The crowd stands and cheers as if the once quiet church mouse has grown into a proud lion. The president looks around the room feeling accomplished but watches as the Chinese and Iranian member turn and head toward the door. The admiral rushes over with some anger and fear heavy on his brow.

"The Chinese and Iranians have chosen to support the Russians and plan on launching their Navies in the Pacific. They are looking to make a squeeze on us, and we don't have enough to defend it. I'm not saying we launch ICBMs, but it may be our only option if we want to hold on to what we have left," says the admiral with some shake in his tone.

"We launch, they launch, and the lives lost will be abominable. I have an idea, on some of the new ships and your Lexington II, do we still have the prototypes of the mounted rail gun?" asks the president.

"Yeah, but they have never been battle tested. Hell I think their concept is more fantasy than reality drawn up by nerds during session of dungeon and dragons. I don't want us to go down with experimental technology. There has to be a better way!" says the admiral strictly.

"Daniel, I love you, and I would want nothing more than to have you by my side for one more battle, but I need you. I need you as my voice, my eyes, and ears out there. More than anything, I need you to have faith in me, to trust me and know that in all I do, it's the lives of everyone I will put before my own. Please get out there because we are stronger with you than without you, and if we have any chance, it's with you in the helm," says the president with a loving grin.

He reaches out to the admiral for a strong and spirited hug and stares at him as if saying goodbye forever. The admiral moved by the emotion gazes back with a swollen tear trying to break the surface of his experienced eyes. He turns and walks quickly toward the door and with blurred vision turns for the last time to the president and says, "I won't let you down!"

Chapter 25

His eyes burn from reading page after page of a weathered and faded New Testament. Sophia rubbing her eyes from her vital sleep rests her chin on Vinnie's shoulder showing affection and interest in what he is doing.

"What are you reading?" asks Sophia as she plays with the hairs on the back of his neck.

"It's 1 and 2 John of the New Testament, and I knew something of this seemed too familiar," says Vinny with some elation.

"What is familiar?" says a more interested Sophia.

"The antichrist, the lies and all. It was already written thousands of years ago," says Vinny.

"What the hell is the antichrist?" asks a now more intrigued Sophia.

"The Bible talks about the second coming of Christ and the battle with the antichrist. Look, Matthew 24:24 says, 'For false messiahs and false prophets will appear and produce great signs and omens, to lead astray, if possible, even the elect,' or this in the book of Revelation 13:11–17, 'Then I saw another beast that rose out of the earth; it had two horns like a lamb and it spoke like a dragon. It exercises all the authority of the first beast on its behalf, and it makes the earth and its inhabitants worship the first beast, whose mortal wound had been healed. It performs great signs, even making fire comedown from the heaven to earth in the sight of all; and by the sign that it is allowed to perform on behalf of the beast, it deceives the inhabitants of earth, telling them to make an image for the beast that had been wounded by the sword and yet lived; and it was allowed to give breath to the image of the beast so that the image of the beast could even speak and cause those who would not worship the image of the beast to be killed. Also it caused all, both small and great, both rich and poor, both free and slave, to be marked on the right hand or the forehead, so that no one can buy or sell who does not have the mark, that is, the name of the beast or the number of its name." Its seems to me that this event was no accident, and the glowing mark and symbol on Ethan's hand could be the mark of the beast like it reads. Sophia, all they are saying and doing almost word for word was forecasted in the New Testament thousands of years ago. This holy war is not new either. Over here is the writing of the Mahabharata that is the transcripts of the Hindu faith. It shows that a great war between two species with amazing power battled each other displaying magnificent weapons. Like all battles, there is a winner and loser, and the loser was cast out to the abyss. In Christianity, they tell a story similar of the fallen angel where a jealous angel goes against God and is cast out to the lakes of fire in hell. This all seems crystal clear, and the one thing that isn't clear is who are the winners. Was it us or another species? So I looked a little more, and there are detail of the watchers and ancient transcript talking about the Anunnaki, a group of deities in ancient Mesopotamia that had awesome power and taught mankind language and math and that's what gave the gift to the Asuras, Amun's ancestors. What if the Anunnaki were the winners and cast out Amun and his species, but it doesn't say what happened to them," Vinny finishes as if to try and catch his breath.

Sophia steps back and stares up and into nothing as if looking for guidance. She breathes a hard exhale and says, "Your persistence of truth is mending. Your faith is inspiring. Vinny, I have something to tell you—"

Her reveal is cut off as Amun walks in and says, "It's time. I need you three to escort me to meet the world's leaders. In this coming moment, we all must judge this world and decide its fate."

Amun turns and walks away looking for them to be in tow. Vinny nervous about his new revelation hesitates but realizes that his only hope of getting to the surface relies on him joining Amun. He tugs on the arm of Sophia and says, "Keep close. I need you with me."

Sophia smiles and turns her head hiding the tear that slowly trickles down her cheek. Ethan quickly comes up the rear anxious teamed with energy and vigor, "You ready for the big reveal, man? This is exciting. You're not still hung up on the bullshit right. This is it the moment, and I have to tell you, man, you're either with us or against us," says Ethan with wide eyes.

"I had no idea there was an ultimatum Ethan. I am also surprised you have turned your back on me so quickly," says Vinny with riled tone.

"Whatever, brother. There are always two sides, and I am picking the winners!" shouts Ethan.

In an effort to lighten the tone, Vinny says, "Just like you pick the Red Sox right," in a playful manner.

"What the hell are you talking about?" snaps Ethan. "What the hell are the Red Sox?"

Vinny stares as if he had just fallen into a delusion brought on by exhaustion and stares in confusion as he enters a room where a massive ship lays waiting. He watches as Yhovah briskly walks over to Amun and says, "The Russians are attacking our ships and demand a meeting."

"Hold them off. Toy with their mediocre technology until I speak with the other world leaders," demands Amun, as he finishes looking at Vinny and Sophia. "We must hurry."

Yhovah walks over to the huge room filled with the simulators and says something in what appears their native language. The room lights up with dark reds, and all the creatures lying in the simulators roar with a menacing sound like barbarians going into battle.

The unsettling noise startles Sophia and Vinny as they make way toward the grand ship awaiting. Vinny seeing the wide entrance gets eager to get as far away as possible from this once magical place.

Rushing into the craft, Vinny looks to where he can sit when Sophia reaches to him and says, "When we get out of here, I have to tell you something."

The doors close, and they sit as the ship prepares to launch.

Chapter 26

The Atlantic is familiar to the admiral as they go to head off the Russians holding true to the president's orders and the request by his friend. The cool crisp winter air rushes his tired face as the land behind them becomes obscure and the landscape he rushes to he knows to be uninviting. The admiral calls out to the captain who comes from the bridge and stands at attention reflecting years of proud discipline.

"At ease, Captain. What is the inventory?" asks the admiral.

"Sir, we have ten battle-ready ships loaded at their maximum with ammunitions. We have three aircraft carriers fully stocked with F-35's, F-18's, and a ghost squadron of the F-23 scorpions. We have five subs all attack ready, three are nuclear ready, and five ships including the Lexington II have prototype aluminum rounds set and ready for the modified rail guns. Sir, why aluminum rounds and not the standard rounds tested?" asks the captain.

"Magnets, Captain, magnets. The president thinks that alien crafts have magnetic pulses, and aluminum cannot be affected, and it will move three times faster. Besides, he wouldn't feel comfortable having me attack aliens from another fucking world or Russians with tested rounds. Nope, he prefers this untested rounds supported by untested rail guns and a ghost squad of F-23's. Captain, what the hell is a F-23?" asks the admiral in a sarcastic tone.

"Ay, Admiral, what is a F-23?" responds the captain.

The two veterans of the sea hint of amusement when their faces turn impassive as the sea glows of unnatural colors and the silhouettes of a massive Russian fleet plagues the background. Soon, a massive pop is heard as two SU-57 fighters cut between the Lexington II and a neighboring battleship causing sailors to hit the deck. The alarms ring out as the admiral yells everyone to their battle stations. The admiral watches, as the Russian fighters break hard and engage on two of the alien crafts closest to them using their guns. The alien spade fighters shimmer from the protective shield and break formation diving toward the ocean in an almost complete ninety-degree angle.

"They couldn't pull up in time at that speed," says the admiral.

The two spade fighters, only two hundred yards from the ocean, pull up and come to almost a complete stop creating a swell ten feet high beneath them. The alien fighter waits as if to taunt the SU-57's that has now taken a tactical position behind the crafts. Instantly, the two spade fighters dart forward to incredible speeds pressing the SU-57's engines to their max. The eerie sounds of the guns echo off the ships as water splashes around the spade fighters that seem unthreatened. The two spade fighters drop below fifty yards above the ocean and maneuver left to right as the rounds continue to do nothing but litter the ocean surface. They all begin to bank left when a whistle is heard as the stealth SU-57 opens a bay door firing an air-to-air missile destined for an alien kill. The savage missile eager to meet the target races at remarkable speeds closing in on the toying spade fighter that now has begun to dive. As the missile nears impact, the spade fighter dives into the ocean at an unimaginable speed forcing the missile to splash down into the ocean flipping and turning breaking apart like a toddler throwing a tantrum for not getting their way. In a flash, about five hundred yards away, the same spade fighter emerges out of the water facing the villainous SU-57, and brilliant flashes of pink energy riddle the plane dismantling it with flashes of fire and debris. The other SU-57 relentlessly trails the second spade fighter whom equally flies casual as if bored by the insignificant bug bothering it. The spiritless spade fighter seems to pull ahead, and the chromed orb energizes it with a blue or purple bolt of energy like lightning, and quickly, the craft seems to cloak showing only a transparent etch of the craft that's almost hard to see with your naked eye. It reflects of the environments around it making it hard to tell where the ocean ends and the fighter starts, as it thrusts twice the speed of the hunting SU-57. The spade fighter well ahead of the SU-57 breaks at almost 180 degrees and comes head-on at the flustered Russian as if playing a game of chicken. The SU-57 unloads all of its armaments in a desperate attempt to down the imposing spade fighter. As flashes of teal and pink reflect off the cloaked fighter unfazed by the vicious weapons, you see a burst of speed from the spade fighter, and it turns back to the matted metal color showing its vintage character. You see from the formation, it's dedicated in its path as is the SU-57, and in an instant, the two collide spreading a huge burst of kinetic energy sending a percussion wave 360 degrees shaking the ships around it. As the debris clears and the smoke and fire mellows, you hear the spade fighter turn and watch as the unscathed alien craft taps the wings from left to right into the ocean like a playful child. It pulls up and quickly blends back into the ranks as if the moment was a break from the discipline of the grid, and soon, it's hard to tell from the others which two spade fighters were the murderous ones. The admiral is taken back by the technology and calls into the president to report of the newfound knowledge.

"Terence, we are in a shit load of trouble. We can't even pretend to have this kind of technology. Two fighters just toyed with SU-57's as if a child made it. It even flaunted the kill by tapping its wings into the water. They saw *Top Gun*. I'm sure of it, and one of them thought they were Maverick. If the Russians get them on their side, we are done, seriously done!" reports the admiral.

"Relax, all they did was show they are the hostile ones and how primitive they are. They just assured the visitors we are the trustworthy ones. That is assuming they see us as separate and that the Russians aren't representing all of mankind. Shit, they may not care. They may see the Russians as our preferred muscle and see us all as hostiles. Damn it, Daniel. Ready the rail guns!" orders the president as he debates himself.

Chapter 27

The vessel begins to make a casual hum, and small vibrations can be felt beneath everyone's feet.

"Sit with me, Vinny. I would like to discuss more of what will happen when we get in front of the world," asks Amun.

Vinny walks casually over to Amun as he questions the intent of the familiar alien. Vinny knows this is his way out, and it may be the best way to find out their true intentions. As he passes Ethan, their eyes meet, and for the first time ever, Ethan looks like a stranger, like they never met before.

"Amun, do you mind if ask a few questions? I have barely slept thinking of all this, and perhaps, some guidance from you can ease my mind," says Vinny as if to stroke Amun's ego.

"Of course, I'm sure all this is overwhelming, and you must have a thousand questions. We have some time. Where do we begin?" asks Amun.

"The Anunnaki, once they felt you could pass on this amazing gift, what happens to them?" starts Vinny.

"I don't know. Some say they die out, while others believe they will look for other worlds to gift. I believe they evolve to a higher plain and become more than this," answers Amun as he pinches softly Vinny's skin on his arm.

"How many years beyond us is your technology? Between what we have seen and my strong imagination, we aren't close to your technology," says Vinny.

"You are moments from our technology. It's one moment that someone realizes physics has limits, but true power comes from within. The Anunnaki came to my world and all they controlled, their ships and equipment came from essence, an internal power

115

source mocked by your general public. That energy people have that gives them super strength in times of survival or crisis, those very few who can move objects with their minds or the understanding of auras, and those who play in spirit worlds, that's essence," says Amun.

"So you don't have power sources like reactors or batteries in the vessels?" asks Vinny.

"Careful, Amun." says Yhovah in a quick tone.

"Relax. No, we don't. Our technology taps into our essence, and it's what powers everything. The stronger your essence, the stronger what you control, and it reflects your character. Your essence defines you, and the equipment you use will reflect your essence in color, like your aura table. All shades of red or blues and greens reflect from the user, and some of the most gifted can move that energy, so it can change from aggression to defense or healing. Even our weapons power it based off essence," says Amun.

"Does it come from within like a psychic, powers of the mind?" says Vinny in almost a mocking tone.

"That is what you will need to discover, Vinny. The Anunnaki controlled their essence with such discipline. They taught us relentlessly to feel peace and look into our inner light to reach the true power of essence, but we developed it through science allowing us to tap into it mechanically and by not being spiritual, and it advanced us thousands of years ahead of schedule, but the Anunnaki were angry, and they—"

"Stop. Enough, Amun," interrupts Yhovah.

Amun who seems angered flares up, and two flaps of skin unfold from behind his head curling over giving an image of horns until he calms quickly, and they fold back.

"I'm sorry to anger you, Amun. So judgment, you decide we are not worthy like before. How do you eradicate an entire species?" says Vinny.

"Our history is sensitive and at times not easy, but I am not angry. Please don't see this as mass extinction, Vinny. This is purification. Our technology matched with essence allows us to manipulate many things. Polar shifts and ocean warming will change the face of this planet in thousands of years. It's happening as we speak, but we can do in a matter of minutes. Your whole world cleansed by massive floods of a diseased infestation," firmly says Amun.

"So you can shift the whole planet in minutes? And what do you mean diseased?" asks Vinny.

"Vinny, to assure purification, we have a process that starts with plague. Let me show you," Amun stands.

"In these pods are reapers, a soulless being that inhabit the earth spreading a biological disease targeting specific DNA codes. They have no regret or sympathy and target the chosen. They live off death and chaos and cannot be allowed to exist unmanaged for long. The purge of this planet with the great floods and shifts cleanses not only the diseased and dying but also the reapers. They are dark, and they have unmatched essence that reflects black in all they consume. We have twelve ships where earth's future inhabitants will wait out the chaos safe from the disease and the reapers. These tribes are meant to carry twelve thousand per ship times twelve, and that's your 144,000 purified human being, the ones who will be granted the honor of spreading the gift of life beyond here. They wait for judgment on the ocean floor in a city we call Judah," says Amun as if impressed.

"Are you saying twelve tribes of Judah? Reapers like grim reapers? Great floods like Noah? This has been done before and warns us of it happening again!" says Vinny.

"Yet here we are. Even with all the warnings, nothing has changed, still a primitive diseased species focused only on self-preservation like a life-raping parasite!" shouts Yhovah.

"So you have already judged us. The jury is out, and we get the death penalty, and either we comply with your decision, or we die in a disease-ravished hell cleansed by a polar shift that ensures whatever survives faces a gruesome death of flood and watery graves!" shouts back Vinny.

In that moment, Vinny feels a sharp pain consume the left side of his head, and his body falls to the floor. Dazed, he sees Ethan getting shoved by Sophia.

"You asshole, you didn't have to hit him!" screams Sophia as she scratches at Ethan's throat.

Ethan not amused grips her shoulders and throws her to the ground, knocking her unconscious.

"We have to secure her for now. She is Anunnaki!" says Yhovah.

Vinny barely able to look up feels blood trickle from behind his head from the cowardice blow. The room seems to shrink and becomes dark as all he hears in head is "she is Anunnaki."

Chapter 28

The flames burn on the surface of the ocean of the now incinerated SU-57's, and within moments, a broadcast is picked up by the American fleet.

"To all parties listening, this vicious attack was initiated by the US government. The Russian Navy was deemed the most powerful armed force, and we were asked to attack the foreign entity that proved to be severely more advanced. These actions should reflect the cowardliness of the United States of America and its allies and not of the nation of Russia or its allies. We ask to join forces with the visiting species in efforts to subdue all aggressive parties who have nuclear capabilities and have shown zero regret for the mass genocide of innocent civilians before. We welcome any foreign entity to meet with Russian leaders to form a truce and to formulate a plan to ensure the earth's survival."

The broadcast attaches images of several videos displaying nuclear disasters from World War II and specifically touches the aftermath of Hiroshima and Nagasaki.

"Well, this is some serious bullshit," screams the admiral as he picks up the phone to the president. "Terence, this is bad. They cut me off at the knees. If I attack their fleet, we look guilty, and if we attack the aliens, we look guilty. Do I just sit and wait and hope the aliens call bullshit?" asks the admiral.

"Power down the weapons and prove to be venerable. There are reports that a large vessel is headed to the UN, and I am banking that someone of power is on board. I have to believe that if they have been here for thousands of years, then they are well aware of the nation's capabilities and any travesty brought on by war. In the event they see a nuclear warhead as a viable threat, then any nations with its power is a threat. On the other hand, to be the only nation that used the weapon in war, we may be seen as the best race to represent mankind. I pray that if they meant to be hostile, then we would have felt their technology already," replies the president.

Ground troops smother the exterior of the UN lawn and show an aggressive presence in the streets of New York City. The grids of spade fighters hum as they begin to part making way for an enormous craft approaching. The vessel as large as a city block hovers only a couple hundred feet above the UN building as all military weapons aim in its direction. A large opening exposes the inside of the warm blue hue from under the vessel, and the grid of spade fighters tilt ninety degrees aiming at the crowd of military personnel. The spheres begin to vibrate and glow and at once flash making the hairs on the people's arms below stand up. Then every single piece of electrical equipment dies forcing all weapons to lock up and malfunction. Even the handheld rifles have ceased giving no room for misfire. The blue interior starts to extend, and with arms wide open, Amun starts to descend from the craft. Yhovah to his side comes to a soft rest on the grass, and the blue hue disappears. Amun with his arms still open mutters a line that most expect.

"I come in peace!" shouts Amun.

Several soldiers lower their weapons, and as Amun lowers his hands to his sides, thousands of the clone warriors appear as if cloaked. They stand there menacing with battle armor and very advanced weapons in their hands. Amun continues to quote from a stereotypical fifties movie and asks kindly, "Take me to your leaders," and begins to walk toward the entrance of the UN.

Everyone seems on edge as Amun makes his way into the UN, and younger soldiers seem to shake as the aggressive clones growl at the weapons aimlessly pointing in all directions.

Inside, the world leaders sit in awe of Amun's presence as they try to see if his character shows any sign of intent. Growls come from the clones insisting the crowd to make way for their leader as he heads toward the podium with the president. The president stares into the sunken ancient face of Amun, and as if to welcome his wisdom, his face demands and puts his hand out.

"We welcome you in peace to the UN where the world is eager to hear your words," says the president as he steps back giving space to Amun, and agents destined to protect him quickly engulf him.

The room, eerie in silence, waits as Amun seems to choose his words carefully, and he reaches his hands high in the air and says, "I am the alpha and the omega. I stand before you not as an equal but your creator. This world has become diseased by greed and lies, and it needs to be cleansed. Thousands of years ago, we came to this planet with a gift, a gift of life and prosperity. Your species was chosen to evolve and add to the meaning of life and pass it on for eternity. The very core of who you are has challenged the very future of life and the millions of species it shares within you. You fight over religion and power. You rape the world you inhabit to fuel your weapons and hate. The very essence of life has no meaning, not of a mother or child or fellow man. You look through your weapons and see only hate and desire to eradicate anyone who disagrees with you. Your foundation is weak and brittles and crumbles, and even while you lay in a garden of debris, you will stand up and claim your passion and beliefs. God is your pedestal that makes you feel righteous. It's the name that gives you meaning for your atrocities. God lets you rape and kill children? God allows you to destroy cities and lives of the innocent. God accepts greed and profit at the expense of health and goodwill? Your god accepts this as long as it's in his name. You believe god to be that self-centered? Allah, HaShem, Krishna, the Father, Son, and Holy Ghost, these are some of your gods. What is god? Is it the being that created you, nurtured you, and in the end will judge you? When you die, you'll stand before them and be judged, and as long as you murdered, raped, stole, and lied in their name, you will receive the gift of heaven and everlasting life. I am here to tell you that by that definition, I am your god, and you insult the very essence of the true god. The primitive apes that walked this earth was given our DNA to grow within them, and our DNA was created by billions of other species blessed with the gift of life and who chose their predecessors. We gave you language, mathematics, science, and agriculture and watched as you evolved into a freethinking civilization. Like proud parents, we nurtured you and stood side by side through your growth, but soon, the ape inside you showed its alpha side, and you began to crumble. Four times, we were forced to judge mankind, and in judgment, we were forced to destroy what we grown to love. The risk of having the wonderful gift of life tainted by one race is unacceptable. To allow humanity, as it is today to extend life, would destroy the very fabric of not only previous life but also its very possibility of ever extending, and that cannot be tolerated. If judgment does not come in your favor, then 144 specific DNA patterns will be chosen to inhabit a new world, and we will purge the earth with disease and disaster allowing this planet to heal, and we will have nature take back control and any life that evolves. This future being of humanity will be created in the purest form set by the one true almighty god that carries no name and just is."

Amun turn and bows his head to show appreciation for the time allowed to talk and begins to walk off among rumblings from the crowd.

"Who are you to judge?" shouts one.

"Can we save ourselves from judgment?" shouts another.

"How do we know who is chosen?" another.

"How much time is left?" yet another

Amun closes his eyes as if heartbroken.

"There is no more time. Humanity cannot undo who they are, and the chosen will know. The rest will have to wait. Death to some is glory, to others an empty door, but regardless it's death, and it comes. For some, it will come as you defend the very core of what brought your destruction, and to others, it will be disease and/or disaster, and it will be pain but still death. The true god doesn't not waste and find comfort in the idea that your very essence will be absorbed into the sea of life and distributed again among the infinite galaxies and planets that cherish the gift," finishes Amun.

The room is silent for a moment, as their fate seems written and reality seems sincere. It's then in the sound of silence a voice can be heard strong willed and determined, and with that strength, several heads raise and see the president speak.

"Your words are true and your assumptions warranted, but your judgment is hypocritical. This judgment is flawed because judgment comes from my equal not my creator. No parent turns their back on their child regardless of their flaws. We have witnessed your technology, and though it's advanced, it is as crude as ours. Though accurate, the weapons used are created to destroy, and you possess a weapon that riddles the world with plague and disaster, which makes you ten times the monster we could ever be. You stand here among flawed men and women who only needed to know there was more than the trivial differences. You woke a sleeping giant in humanity that realizes. Unified, we are unstoppable because we fight for not just an inch of land but for all we are. You now showed that god by our simple definition was adolescent at best and that what we fought about was a childhood toy in a shared toy box. You expected with your chosen words and detailed revelation that we would curl up and die as you see fit. You may be the alpha and the omega, but we are the apes determined to live. We accept your horror of death and disaster and fear none of it because what is our core is pride, sir. Pride creates warriors. Powerful determined warriors and united proud warriors from all corners of the globe will win or by our god die trying!" shouts the president as he slams his hand on the podium.

The grounded room roars in approval as they understand a hero has emerged, and Amun makes his way toward the door.

By the exit, Amun turns and says, "Wonderful speech but meaningless. It has begun. Doubt is evident in this room, and the chosen will be notified. You have support at this moment, but what will happen when they realize they are chosen, will they support you then or run to my arms in fear of death? What will happen when death knocks over and over again and their loved ones suffer? What will happen as walls of water a thousand feet high eradicate city after city or when the earth splits swallowing it whole? They will remember you and the mere man who defied a god and who brought anguish to their children and mothers. You, Terence, will be the face of pain and death, and you will be hated by millions," calmly spits back Amun who taps his chest as all clones. Yhovah and himself cloak and seem to vanish as the craft pulls away.

The president dismisses the ground and asks to meet in twelve hours to discuss options with the supporting crowd and as they leave says only one simple thing, "Those of you not strong enough to fight for humanity must turn your back on all it has surpassed. Judgment comes from the almighty and a mirror nothing else. If you're not here when we begin in twelve hours, you will not be judged by anyone other than the mirror you stare at, but I will not lay down chosen or not at the destruction of billions of innocent human beings."

Chapter 29

Vinny feels the thumping of his heartbeat on the side of his head, and in a means to ease his suffering, he feels fingers brushing through his hair. Dazed, he looks up and in a blur sees the warm face of Sophia who stares back with concern.

"Are you okay?" asks Sophia.

"No, I was sucker punched by my best friend and lied to by a woman I thought to be an angel. This sucks!" says Vinny.

He sits up and sees they are still in a ship and are contained by the same type of bubble that saved them days before.

"We don't have much time, so you need to listen, and this is going to be a lot, so please just shut your mouth and open your ears okay?" says Sophia.

Vinny conflicted seems to want to debate her but feels that her words are important to his understanding of everything going on.

"Okay," says Vinny.

"I am Annunaki. We have existed for millions of years, and we are the keepers of life and the watchers of this planet and all mankind. Almost eighty million years ago, my ancestors went to a water world deemed a candidate for life. Probes found a primitive aquatic life-form that had qualifying DNA samples needed for the gift of life. Like all candidate planets, we go and generate samples of evolving life-forms with an early stage of DNA manipulation. This is stage one. The Asuras were magnificent. They absorbed knowledge like a sponge and evolved faster than any species before it. We teach the same cores to every species, but science and mathematics seemed to accelerate in their core genetics. The creators were so impressed with their advancement that they thought they could advance them outside the standard time frame. This was a huge mistake, as we learned, that the process of DNA insertion has been perfected billions of years before, and the specific time line has purpose. The core to stage five, which is what level the Annunaki possess, is the use of essence. Essence as Amun told you is the energy that creates your soul and fuels your existence. It is deep within you and is limitless, and through deep harmony of mind, soul, and spirit, it can be controlled and harnessed. When tapped into, it creates energy to move objects, powers vehicles, and at times powers weapons as well as heal and regenerate. Your character, what makes you you, is what determines what kind of vehicle you create or colors of light emitted for your dwelling or the power of your weapon. Its power is intoxicating, and only level five entities should be taught to use it. The Asuras were evolving at such a rate. They were level three 40 percent faster than any other species before. The elders taught them essence, and soon, the problem was evident. They wanted that power now, and they grew impatient, so instead of finding essence, they created it through science bypassing thousands of years set aside for level four. They determined that essence though deemed spiritual was still scientific and must have a formula. They were correct, but when not being used through the harmony of mind, spirit, and soul and abusing the science, it drains your essence, and it sucked their life from their core, and they would die. We tried to slow them down and explained that using the science of essence and not learning the proper process would spell certain doom for their species, but it was too late. They evolved so fast that our wisdom and experience had no value, and they continued on their own. The elders soon felt the continued gift of life was no longer a viable option, and the Asuras were considered an aborted species. The Asuras were livid with the elder's decision and demanded we leave immediately, and so we charted a new path set by probes that lead us to earth. In the process of charting and preparing, the now very advanced Asuras found a way to hack our probes and see the charted path to Earth. They vowed to disrupt the process of DNA transfer to Earth and the further spread of life and with their advanced technology raced ahead to meet the primitive species that was meant to replace them. This was now a major problem. As Annunaki, we are sworn to the progress of life and now earth, but now we have a species that advanced too far and with hostile intent plan on disrupting all life. Every attempt to seed the earth was thwarted by the Asuras creating abominations of nature and unqualified for level one. They never received the needed process to reach level four which taught them the DNA transfer methods, and they continued to create beings coded incorrectly but yet insisted on being an Annunaki replacement. The elders knew it needed to stop and set out to stop the Asuras after three purges were needed to cleanse the earth of their failed creations. The war of the heavens was our attempt to eradicate the Asuras from Earth and from all of history. The obsession of essence had destroyed the Asuras on their home planet, which now lies dead in a distant galaxy. The last essence was used to send twelve ships to Earth, and what traveled to Earth was all that remains from a dead world. They perfected clones and create them for soldiers and for essence and during the battle of the heavens used all they had to combat us. The problem is that true essence cannot be depleted, and soon their crafts failed, and soon their species died off, and Amun and Yhovah Amun's son are all that remains. They look the way they do from the battles and the essence that was taken from them and now turned their science on humanity. They now are looking to gene splicing that would merge human DNA with theirs creating a hybrid Asuras like the child you saw when we first arrived. This could not happen, and the battle was enormous, spanning over one-hundred fifty years all across the globe. Humanity was catapulted into what they called a holy war exposing all the technology both the Asuras and we had. The Asuras took to the human interpretation of our technology as divine, and the Asuras placed themselves in positions of power, divine power. They labeled themselves as living gods and soon embedded themselves into mainstream society manifesting themselves as kings, emperors, and pharaohs all while sharing technology with primitive man only to erect massive monuments to honor them. The influence was global and as their essence wore away and we defeated them and eventually banished them to the abyss. They are dying and are desperate for the hybrid species to mature so they can inhabit the earth. In the last one hundred years, they have amassed an army of clones in the billions, but their essence is maybe a quarter of the original Asuras, and they die quickly. Their influences have been monitored and believed to have played a role in the rise of the Nazis and may be why they were so advanced compared to other nations. We have quietly kept them at bay hoping that they would die off without incident because with your advanced state, this next war of heavens would kill millions. We now stand here with them exposed as a last attempt to harness the earth and mankind, and we have to stop them for the last time," says Sophia with a sigh of relief.

Vinny stares at her with such wonder and amazement as he tries to absorb all that was revealed, and he opens his mouth, but only a weird squeak comes out.

Sophia giggles and with a smile says, "You have questions?"

"So the Bible and its stories are tales of the battle between you, the Annunaki and the Asuras. The interpretation as being divine was translated into a holy war where you were seen as heavenly and the Asuras were the fallen. They say we are created in God's image, and you look human, more so than Amun and the clones, so why would anyone follow the Asuras?" asks Vinny.

"Power, Vinny. They exposed the very magnificent power of their essence and ships, while we chose to limit our power and exposure, and we were hunted by the Asuras and their followers which developed into stories throughout the Bible," answers Sophia.

"So is God real?" asks Vinny in an almost nervous tone worried of the answer.

"Not the god that has been depicted but something so much more. No entity has direct knowledge of God, and only the dead know of God's existence. God is wonderful, and he created life before time was time, and God created the process of extending life. When you pray, something amazing is listening that cannot be explained but felt, and when someone must define God, label God, or give God a name, then they already are wrong. Religion is the right idea, but humanity needs to see it as a way to celebrate all that life is. Think about it, Vinny. Inside you may be millions and millions of species all sharing a piece of who they are so you can be you. Only something as wonderful as God could create that, so yes, God is real," says Sophia with a small tear dripping from her eye. This is sincere love of life, and it has touched Vinny to the core. He realizes it's not about a title of being Catholic, Christian, or Muslim but sharing your devotion to something wonderful that doesn't need a label. Vinny's lips shiver as he holds in his emotion and soon gathers himself to ask one more question.

"What about you, are you divine or human? Can you love and have a family, or is this just your role within the big picture? Could we be together?" asks Vinny in an embarrassed and broken tone.

"Vinny, we live and die like you, but we live a lot longer. My goal in my time here is to influence mankind to be better, to treat each other better, and to direct you into the path of level two. Yes, we could be together, but as you aged, I would not. We couldn't have a family or stay in any one place too long to avoid suspicion. It wouldn't be a fair life, and if you got sick, I couldn't help even though my technology and essence could heal you. I would have to watch you suffer and die and deal with the pain of losing you, but I would gladly suffer for a thousand years to have five minutes with you," says Sophia as she leans over and kisses Vinny. The kiss was enchanting like the melding of two souls, and Vinny was overwhelmed with love and joy beyond anything he has felt before.

"Now, listen. It's time we bust out of this joint, and we need to get down to my elders and maybe get them to talk with the president cause this is about to get ugly quick. Are you ready?" asks Sophia.

Vinny still in a trance from the kiss looks at her with a funny glaze and says, "Whatever, babe, I'm with you."

Sophia slaps him in a funny way to get his game face on and says, "Focus. It's about to get crazy."

Sophia closes her eyes, and Vinny begins to feel his arm hairs stand up like he has electricity running all around him. He looks over to Sophia who opens her eyes to reveal a bright green glow, and her veins swell in her forearm and hands with the same bright green, and in that instant, she opens her palms, and a burst of energy explodes shattering the bubble and tossing the one clone watching them. The walls are burnt as her essence skips across the room, and all electronics in the room are fried. She reaches down and picks up the guard's weapon, and as soon as her hand touches it, the weapons glows green inside the chambers and hums as if supercharged. A door blasts open, and soon, three clones charge in her direction. Sophia fires a burst of energy at the one in the center and on impact explodes painting the walls in smelly goo.

"I hate that fish smell when they explode," says Sophia in a playful tone without taking her eyes off the other two charging.

Vinny cautiously standing several feet back says, "Would you think less of me if I pissed myself?"

Sophia laughs and begins to run in the clone's direction. One has managed to grasp its thick claws into the walls and run almost parallel on the wall and then lunges at Sophia high as the other goes low. Sophia seems to do a slow front flip firing the weapons into the skull of the lower clone, and as she rotates, her veins begin to glow, and she thrusts the glowing hand into the creatures' chest, and with a loud scream, a burst of energy splits the clone in two. The action was two seconds long but felt like forever to Vinny, but he soon begins to chuckle as a large chunk of the creature is stuck in her hair.

"Damn it!" says Sophia. "I'll never get that smell out of my hair," and with a smile, she grabs his hand that's warm to the touch and brings him into an adjacent chamber where there is a spade fighter.

"What the hell do you think we are going to do with that?" asks Vinny.

"We are going to blast out of this hanger and fly down into the city and hope that the military still doesn't have weapons function and ask to see the president," says Sophia in a calm tone.

"What the fuck you mean hope they don't have weapons, and just say hello to the president? Why don't you just use some of that green essence and zap us down or something?" says Vinny in a nervous tone.

"No, honey. It doesn't work like that. Besides, I haven't eaten in a while, and I'm not sure my essence can block all military weapons and keep the ship from crashing and get us out of this hanger. That's a lot to ask from a girl who just had some fruit and a salad," giggles Sophia.

Vinny just stares like it is too much to comprehend and just follows her to the craft.

Sophia opens the canopy, and there sits a clone in an odd-shaped helmet, and he growls aggressively while trying to bite her. She grabs the visors and rips them from his head as blue–green goo shoots into the cockpit. She reaches into the console and opens the chambers his arms are in and pulls out his arms as more goo flies around the cockpit. She tosses the clone out and sits in the cockpit and asks Vinny to sit on her lap quickly.

"Why all the nasty stuff? Aw it smells so bad (covering his nose)? Was all that tech attached to him?" asks Vinny.

"First they are just really, really smart fish, and two, yes, the science behind the tech and essence is that all those pins in their head and arm tap in their core to extract the essence instead of how I am using mine. To rip them out of the tech releases the essence at once, and they die instantly. It's nasty right?" says Sophia, and as she grips the controls, the entire tech comes alive. The panels read full power, and the craft hovers; the canopy closes, and it's jet black for a second until the whole spade fighter becomes clear.

"Okay, I'm freaking out. why is this clear like a Wonder Woman jet?" asks Vinny.

"It is how it's seen from inside so no blind spots, but on the outside, it looks how you saw it. Are you ready?" answers Sophia.

As Vinny tries to answer, she send off a rapid burst of energy blowing out the wall and exposing the outside. The fighter darts out of the opening and hovers just above Yankee stadium.

"This has to be fate!" shouts Vinny and in that instant feels his stomach drop as Sophia dives the craft toward the deck. She banks hard over the Hudson River and heads toward the UN, and soon, the craft is splashed with red blasts from behind.

"We have one on our tail. Hold on. This is about to get crazy," shouts Sophia.

Sophia dives the fighter toward the river and pulls up only feet from the water splitting the water and creating a mist of water shaped like a vortex. The craft seems to shift from the inside, and the monitor shows a shape change to the hull.

"What the hell is this thing doing?" asks Vinny.

"I like this look better, and it's better underwater!" says Sophia.

"You can just change its shape like that?" asks Vinny.

"It's quasicrystals, like liquid metal, and it's resilient. I can't explain at the moment," answers Sophia.

In that instant, the craft splashes under a dark Hudson River, and the monitor seems to brighten the Hudson floor. Sophia looks up and sees the other fighter keeping pace above and gets an idea.

"Okay, so don't freak out, but we have to get him by surprise. Otherwise, he will mark our location and hundreds from the grid will attack us. With my essence, I can get the craft up fast enough to turn water into a plasma which has little resistance, and he'll still think he is keeping pace. We will bank and come right at him and destroy him before he can blink. Sounds good?" says Sophia.

"Whatever. I'm not a physicist. I will just throw up. Let me know when it's over," says Vinny.

The craft lights up, and soon, the speed underwater starts turning the water into a pearl-like blue, and then instantly, Sophia banks the craft 180 degrees and starts heading toward the incoming fighter.

"See no tolls this was, honey," says Sophia.

"You can't call me honey right now," shouts Vinny who is as green as the essence.

As the gap between the two come together, Sophia pulls up hard, and what seems like slow motion, he sees as the two crafts collide. Sophia now brilliant glow warms the cockpit as they devour the incoming craft, and as the debris clears, more goo is all over the nose of her fighter.

"Bull's-eye! Now I really need to eat," says Sophia as she heads toward the UN. She comes in slow as the military seem be without their weapons still and rest the fighter on the lawn. Several military personnel rush the craft as the canopy opens exposing a beautiful Sophia and a clearly sick Vinny. Vinny jumps out and throws up all over the grass and an officer's shoes, and Sophia with her hands raised says, "I need to see the president, and I need food like now."

Chapter 30

Amun paces in anger as his ship heads out over the Atlantic.

"How dare they question and challenge my divine power! Do they not realize I can destroy them in seconds? The hybrid system needs to be escalated because a war seems inevitable. We will need to be swift, and I think we need to meet with the Russians. We will need pawns to die for our cause and preserve essence. Their lust for power and control will be an easy platform to use. Promise them access to our technology and the right to reign after the purge," orders Amun.

Yhovah plots the Russian's location and presses a mark on a translucent screen. Several clones growl in pain as the pins puncture their hardened skin and tap into their essence.

"We disabled their weapons and have requested to meet on their largest ship," says Yhovah.

"Excellent. I fear the humans will reach out to the Annunaki and gain their support," says Amun.

"You gave a lot of information to Vinny. He will share that with the other leaders, and Sophia will get the Annunaki to support their cause," answers Yhovah.

"Yes, but we have Ethan, don't we?" says Amun as he taps the shoulder of Ethan standing by his side.

The craft comes to a stop above the large aircraft carrier, and Amun and Yhovah head to the deck along with several cloaked clones. They are met by a Russian admiral and an Iranian general both eager to meet with Amun.

"I am Admiral Ivanov, and this is General Hamid, and we are at your service," says Admiral Ivanov.

"Time is limited, Admiral, and I'm going make this quick. The US government has shown the lack of respect expressed in your broadcast. The lack of respect for life here on this planet and the very existence of life as it has been expressed. I am sure you heard my words to the leaders in the UN, and so I offer you this. The purge is evident, and the lasting humans meant to be granted the gift of life was universal. Now in the reflection of defiance, I grant you full access to our technology, and the inherited chosen for mankind will only have Russian and Iranian blood. In return, you will rage war on the US and its allies and eradicate them by all means available to you. The chosen will reign this world without despair or disease, and we will guide you to everlasting life," says Amun.

"Who will reign? The Russians or Iranians? Will they be raised in the teachings of Allah?" asks General Hamid.

The question has the Russian Admiral caught off guard, and he quickly stares at the general as if he has been insulted. The general refusing to make eye contact goes to continue his questions but is interrupted by Amun.

"You dare ask of Allah in my presence, a being I created. Mohamad, Jesus Christ were mere puppets on my strings meant to control the simple minds of humanity. You ask who will reign? The Asuras will reign, and you will bow before for me, and for your loyalty, you will be granted life everlasting, peace, and riches. Your people will know nothing of disease or suffering, hunger or pain, but only of a world of harmony riddles with respect of life. This is the only way to preserve life, and under our guidance, your advancement in the gift of life is assured. I will not tolerate the defiance of our divine nature, and any more mention of false idols will not go without punishment. I am the alpha and the omega, and to question it will be punished by death, death not of the one but of the death of your entire nation. Every last man, woman, or child will kneel or perish. These are my terms, and either agree or feel the wrath of my power, and I will give you a chance to see if your god is real," shouts Amun as the flaps spike up from behind his head forcing a grimacing character. The general in fear drops to his knees followed by the admiral both committing their loyalty to the power and rule of Amun.

"Contact your leaders and be prepared to launch your nuclear warheads at the US and its allies. They cannot be allowed to gather support and muster a defensive. They will look for support from the Annunaki," states Amun.

"Annunaki?" asks the admiral.

"A rogue race set against the expansion of life. They exist to destroy the spread of a master race like the Asuras and will manipulate humans like the US to believe they are for the greater good of humanity. They fear progress and preach relic gospel hoping weak-minded species believe they are watchers of the gift and this earth and claim it takes millions of years to perfect. In the meantime, they hide among societies and live off natural resources tapping into what the planet offers. Once the species has been exhausted, they move on as the species and planet dies. The human race was created as nothing more than slave labor to mine resources and cater to their needs. We came to liberate this species after they destroyed my ancestors and our world. When we tried to educate your species but they fought us, and we retreated into the deep reaches of the ocean where we laid silent and rebuilt our forces. We sat for hundreds of years perfecting hybrids spliced with our DNA to combat the Annunaki, but they destroyed them and erased their existence from any history on this planet, while they continued to influence the slave race they created. They despise the Asura because we were the progress of life. We are superior in every way, and they could not grasp their time was up. They are powerful but are reluctant to use it in fear of your species getting their technology and using it against them. We are dying, Admiral, and soon without our fusion with mankind, you'll be forced to defend this planet alone. They have technology that would wipe this world clean as they have done before to our creations, and we do not have the resources or time. We cannot allow them to destroy our last chance at integration. If we fail at this DNA transfer of your brothers, then not just humanity dies with this world but so does the Asuras and all life before it," states Amun.

"Our devotion is to you, our creator, and we will use our resources to annihilate anything that opposes you. We have vast amounts of weapons, jets, and tanks that is years ahead of any opposing forces, technology, or defenses. We appreciate the blessing of inheriting the earth and supporting your reign and progress of life's gift. However, we have to agree to use nuclear weapons would only provoke the US and its allies to use theirs, and this world would be poisoned. The math says we all have enough nuclear warheads to destroy this world three times over, and I'm sure you do not want to reign a dead world," says General Hamid.

"There is very little time, General. Do as you must, but we will proceed in selecting the chosen throughout your counties when the time comes, and it comes soon. We will destroy all that remains, and the reset of this planet will be set for a united Asura and human hybrid dedicated to the advance of life's gift," responds Amun.

"Our first wave is on its way to striking the east coast. Within days, the world may lay at your feet!" responds the admiral.

The admiral opens his phone and says one word, and the ship becomes alive. The advanced SU-57 engines whistle as each starts making its way toward the top of the flight deck as their first offense takes shape.

"Yhovah, have our fighters escort this first wave, and if they begin to destroy the US's weak defense, have our fighters level the playing field. I want the casualties to be so great on both sides that the only answer is nuclear. This is easier than we thought, and they will destroy each other without wasting what little essence we have left. Start to gather hosts. From what I see, the clone of Ethan seems to be stable, and the Asura's DNA has not been rejected. This may be our Adam!" finishes Amun with an malevolent grin.

Chapter 31

The faces of the anxious soldiers stare ready to fire at any flinch made by Vinny or Sophia. The conference room is littered with diplomats watching as Vinny and Sophia make way to the president who sits blanketed by the secret service. The soldiers scan the room looking for cloaked clones that might silently be in tow but flip their visors when they see they are alone.

"I hear you requested to see me specifically. You have my attention. Where are you from?" asks the president.

"Arthur Ave and E 179 St. Bronx, NY," responds Vinny.

"I think they meant me since I was driving. I'm from E 167 St and Jerome Ave, but way before that, we came from a star system by Orions belt," says Sophia.

"You look nothing like the alien that was here a few hours ago claiming to the almighty himself and swore judgment on a billion people. Are you a female version of his species?" asks the president.

"Yuck, *no*! Please, like I would have kids with a fish, a smart fish, but a fish nonetheless," giggles Sophia.

"I am sorry, but it's been a rough day, and I am not sure anything seems less ridiculous than another," responds the president.

"Why are you here? How did you fly their ship?" screams out from the crowd of diplomats.

The president frustrated with the outburst says, "Quiet!" as he thinks they are fair questions.

"That's a fair question, but the answer is complicated. We are the watchers of your kind and this planet. We have been here longer than time has been recorded or understood. We helped create this world and are the givers of life and oversee the progress of your advancement as we direct you through the five levels. We are the Annunaki!" says Sophia.

"Okay, so the last creature that was here says he is the alpha and omega and by all definitions god. Now you say you're a watcher and giver of life and all because you crashed one of their fighters on the UN lawn. Please, with all due respect, you look as human as any other beautiful woman. Why in the world would we believe you're not just a girl from the Bronx?" says the president with a grin.

"With all due respect, Mr. President, my last few days has been the most traumatic, eye-opening, emotional roller coaster that I could ever have imagined. I was raised in a religious house, and everything I have seen defied all I was taught. The alpha and omega was one true God, my savior and my salvation. I sat freezing with Sophia in the middle of the Atlantic Ocean after Russian rounds destroyed a rescue ship I was on. As I sat there waiting to die, a Russian boat came to rescue Sophia and I from a cold and lonely death. That moment turned to chaos as splinters of wood riddled the plank we were on as the welcome Russian boat became murderous wishing nothing more than to bury and signs of an international incidents," starts Vinny.

"They fired on you, unarmed civilians?" interrupts the president.

"That's nothing. As I waited to be ripped apart by the mounted gun, we were saved by the very species that met with you earlier. They saved our life and a life of a dying friend, a friend I thought I had. They have elaborate cities beneath the ocean that rival anything I have seen on the surface. I watched as they took a friend dying from the blast and made him better than he was before. They have tech ions more advanced than ours that you obviously seen. They believe they are more magnificent than they really are and added with that technology make them dangerous, but that's not what I learned in the few days down there. I learned they are scared. They hide relics of ancient pasts, desecrate the Bible, and challenge God and all he is. I learned that God was more real than I have imagined and life was more of a gift than we understand. I learned that anything that values life shouldn't seek to destroy it but rather nurture it and help it grow. They want to destroy us cause we are the chosen not them, and all we have is Sophia and the Annunaki to help us," finishes Vinny.

"Vinny speaks the truth, Mr. President. The Asuras are gathering support as we speak and most likely convincing the Russians and their allies to attack. For several millennia, the Asuras have been trying to create a master race that is merged with their DNA. They have created several species that were genetic abominations that we were forced to destroy. They have influenced humanity to murder each other in the name of god and nation giving rise to monsters like Hitler. They have very little time left, and this last attempt will be the most challenging. This battle will decide not only humanities' fate but also the very fate of future life. The council agrees, if the Asuras succeed in overtaking humanity and have control of all future advancement of this species, we have no choice but to destroy all life on this planet. We will have to start all over again and move on to another place and another species at level one. This is our responsibility, and it offers no option of reason or debate," says Sophia in a saddened tone.

"So what options do we have? We clearly don't have technology to fight them! Can we expect support from you and your species?" asks the president.

"Mr. President, this is all new to us. We have no rules in play for a rogue species battling for supremacy and the right to expand their DNA. The rules are to nurture a species and not be involved after a specific level. We are allowed to influence or make very minor entrances to maybe help along, but what you need is a complete melding of our species, and I just don't know what my elders feel is best," says Sophia.

"Let me go to them with Vinny and see if they can understand the severity of the issue. I will be back in two days with support, and if I come alone, Mr. President, I will die defending your race. That's a promise," finishes Sophia.

"Where are you going?" asks the president.

"Peru, to our lake where the council resides and my father Enki leads our people. His wisdom and understanding will direct us all, and if I return with him, it will assure humanity of victory over the Asuras," says Sophia as she heads toward the door looking for Vinny to follow.

"Mr. President, I believe in you and what you stand for, but I believe in all of mankind, and I will talk to the Annunaki and hope they see my passion and desire for love and unity and in so gain their support, or die trying, sir," says Vinny as he walks with Sophia.

"Mr. President, the admiral is calling and says it's urgent," says a staff member.

Covering his hand over the phone the president says, "Hold on for two minutes. This may be important. What's up, Daniel? Is everything okay?"

"No, sir, we have several reports from some recon planes showing movement from both Iran and Russian militaries. A full Russian navy battle group is headed our way supported by the Iranians, and there is report of nuclear movement. Activity has been reported for both intercontinental ballistic sights, and four submarines are now not in port which all house several nuclear missiles each. We are at war, Terence, and this is a war that will end all wars. To make this worse, several of the alien crafts, big ones, are in tow, and thousands of the spade fighters are circling them. I'm scared shitless, and you can put that on the report I don't care, but we are about to get an ass whipping unless you have something I don't know about," states the admiral.

"Okay, I have some ideas, but I want you to activate the Scorpion Ghost Squad and ready the rail guns. I hope in the next forty eight hours, we will have some aliens of our own!" says the president as he grins at Vinny and Sophia waving them to get going.

"Okay, one, what the fuck is a Scorpion Ghost Squad, and two, what do you mean our own aliens? Seriously, Terence, what the fuck are you talking about? Have you lost your goddamn mind?" shouts the admiral.

"Trust me, I will send the info to you now through our secure network. Have those systems engage as soon as they are in range and report on the damage, and stop cursing so much," replies the president.

"Make it happen, son," says the president to himself as Vinny and Sophia get back in the ship.

Sophia still stuffing her face seems to satisfy her hunger and looks at Vinny and says, "Okay, so it might get weird, and we have to get there fast. You up for it?"

"What do you mean weird? More weird than you glowing green aliens in the ocean and World War III never mind the smart fish?" replies Vinny.

"Yes!" replies Sophia as she grips the controls and her hands begin to glow teal and pink.

Chapter 32

"Okay, Captain, the president has asked me to trust him, and so I will even though he lost his freaking mind. I should be receiving an encrypted file, and it should be describing a ghost squad called Scorpions. We need to make sure that the rail guns are charged, and from what I know of Terence, he believes a good defense is a strong offense," starts the admiral as he hangs up the phone.

"Yes, sir. I will call the ghost squad pilots to the briefing room now while you read the file, and based on what you said, we should be in range within two hours," says the captain.

"You know what the fuck the ghost squad is? How the hell am I out of the loop? Okay, I see the file now. I will be down in twenty minutes," says the admiral as he opens the curious file.

The file opens with the president making an opening statement to the admiral.

"Sorry, buddy, I didn't want you out of the loop on this one, and I know you're probably pissed, but this isn't even a system that has been battle tested, but below is the detailed report of the Scorpion Ghost Squad."

Soon, images of a seventh-generation stealth fighter appear, and a voice begins to describe in detail what the fighters are capable of.

"The F23 Scorpion is the first plasma-based engine tested originating from the Aurora project. The fighter is capable of over Mach 6 and houses two hypersonic nuclear missiles, ten air-to-air combat missiles, and a modified Gatling rail gun and as a defense weapons holds a combat laser capable of downing missiles from over ten miles away. This fighter is unmanned, and it will allow the pilots to exceed any limitations usually held captive by manned fighters."

The file continues to broadcast specific details and images of weapons tests and aerial maneuvers, which make the admiral smile with some confidence.

"Okay, Daniel, this is my trick in a bag and for your eyes only. In the nineties, we developed space needles, and they mimic communication satellites to avoid detection. I have attached a detailed analysis of a space needle striking in the Atlantic, its blast radius and after effects. This won't win the war but maybe buy us time to either find a resolve or gain some possible new support. I wish you well, my friend, and know you're the man for this. You're my friend, my brother, and expect you home to tell me the look on those bastard's faces. I love you, fam," closes the president.

"Admiral, it looks like we underestimated the time frame, radar picks up a massive fleet of crafts maybe two hundred miles straight ahead," reports an officer as the admiral comes to the bridge.

It's cold, and smoke lifts off the water and dances like children at a skating rink. There is tension in the air as the admiral feels the Russians lurking in the morning haze. In the distance, the sun breaks the horizon giving life to all the sunlight touches. The ocean changes from black to blue, and the warming sunlight shimmers of the breaking waves. Seagulls begin to dance in the air eager to find anything to eat, and the melody of their song beckons the start of the day.

"This is my favorite part of the day," says the admiral as he sips from his steaming cup of coffee.

The admiral enjoys this moment because in the distance, he sees the faint silhouette of the Russian fleet and knows the day will not end the way it has started.

"Great day to die huh, Captain?" asks the admiral.

"Yes, sir," replies the captain, "just not sure who's doing the dying."

"I'm ready to die for my family, my friend, and my country and take as many of these bastards with me," states the admiral. "Let's make it so, Captain."

The Captain sets of the all hand's alarm and makes the call to all surrounding ships, and within moments, the roar of F-35's and F-18's litter the air. The ships break apart in to three groups going left, right, and up the middle, and soon a splash is heard as subs break the surface. The Lexington II comes full ahead, and an eerie hum rings from the deck as they power up the rail gun.

"Sir, the system is charged and ready, and the ammunition is loaded. We targeted the carrier, and it's locked. The estimated damage is rated at 80 percent. It will sink," says the lieutenant.

"Okay, full stop all ships. The president has a surprise. Please broadcast the message and launch the ghost squad," orders the admiral.

As the broadcast transmits, the once warming sun grows dark as the sky seems flooded with a swarm of aircraft.

"Sir, there has to be a thousand planes and alien craft coming our way. We have maybe five minutes," says the lieutenant.

"Great day to die," says the admiral with a menacing grin.

As the fog lifts, the Atlantic fleet becomes evident, and the crew seems startled as they see the American Navy has no intentions of backing down.

"I wish you well. Make this quick. There is not much time left before judgement, and these defiant savages need to be eradicated," shouts Amun has he enters the ship eager to avoid the fight.

"What of the Chinese?" asks Yhovah.

"They have put their faith in their empty gods and accept judgment. They walked away from the fight and refused to support either side. They have noted that they will defend their territory and only their territory," states Amun. "I admire their idea but pity their results. They too will die. Yhovah, when our ships reach the half way point, lets block them from any communications and have all our crafts dive. Let's see what happens when big brother doesn't have their back!"

Soon, the whistle of SU-57's scream through the air and guns circle to aim at the incoming fleet.

"We have a broadcast coming through," shouts a bridge officer.

"This is the president of the United States of America, and we issue this warning," starts the president. "We are a proud and confident nation but a compassionate and compromising one as well. We would like to offer you the choice to cease and desist in your attack and risk the lives of thousands of your military personnel. In the event you don't heed our warning, I have authorized the use of every weapon available unleashing hell on your forces. Make no mistake. We have allowed you to see what we wanted you to see, and you severely underestimate our technology and power and—"

"This ridiculous propaganda is insulting, a mere desperate attempt to a dead nation before we erase their name from history," giggles Admiral Ivanov as he lift his finger from the broadcast button cutting off the president's warning.

"They are splitting," shouts a deck hand. "Three ships are punching the middle, but their deck cannons look odd," he finishes.

"Focus all craft and weapons on those three ships. These are command vessels, and we will take off the head of the monster, and the body will fall. We may be having dinner in Central Park by tomorrow," says Admiral Ivanov.

The planes and alien fighters darken the sky and head toward the front ships like angry wasps protecting their nest. The weapons are armed, and they are minutes from an air campaign never seen by a military in the history of mankind.

"Sir, our communications are down, and we have no contact with the ships," says one of the pilots.

"No problem. Our orders are clear. It's probably interference from the alien technology. Get ready to engage," says the commanding pilot.

Just as the pilots are ready to engage, the alien fighters dive hard and splash into the ocean. The once menacing swarm now appears manageable and soon sees an equal air campaign in their direction. Within moments, SU-57's start to explode as missiles riddle the fighters. The stealth fighters are coming from both sides and head-on, and they were undetected by radar.

"They came out of nowhere, and they seem cloaked. They have no cockpit," shouts a pilot.

The pilot watches as a blue glow bursts from each of the ships and a warhead rips across the ocean making the water rip apart and scar.

"What the fuck was that?" shouts a pilot as they bank hard away from the threat.

"Oh my god," shouts another pilot as the impact from the cannon splits the ships in two including the lead aircraft carrier.

"Was that a rail gun?" shouts a pilot.

"Can they fire ag—" starts another as a blinding light interrupts them.

"They have no idea what's about to happen. Prepare all crafts for heavy seas and flooding. After the first stealth attack, have all fighters jump to thirty thousand feet and wait. Lieutenant, on my mark, get ready to fire that rail gun," orders Admiral Gray.

"Fire," orders the admiral, and an electric whistle explodes as the aluminum rounds launch toward the Russian elite aircraft carrier.

"Holy shit, look at that!" shouts the lieutenant as the rounds part the ocean like the Red Sea. The impacts buckle the entire port side of the ship splitting it in two. The massive explosion sends a percussion across the ocean felt by the American fleet mirrored by the two other ships that receive the same fate. The Russian ships as well as the Iranian's start to turn to avoid impacts. The submarines start to dive as the ocean begins to get littered with sailors from the sinking ships.

"Get me the phone," shouts the admiral. "Okay, Terrence, the show is yours."

"Okay, this might buy us the time we need to gain support. Are your ships ready for the storm? Waves are estimated at forty feet maybe higher," asks the president.

"Great day to die, my friend. We are ready," answers the admiral.

The president hesitates and then pushes the button, and soon, a flash is seen hitting the area where the Russian fleet was fleeing. The light is brilliant, and soon, a wind picks up, and a mushroom cloud surrounds the area that the fleet was in.

"Are you fucking kidding me, we nuked them?" says an ensign.

"No for almost twenty years we have been working on a project called Thor. What you witnessed was one god rod dropped at almost thirty thousand miles an hour, and the kinetic energy and the atmosphere cause the fire ball. No fallout, no radiation, just roughly a one hundred city block radius of USA-made ass kicking. Now hold on to your butts because that water has to go somewhere," says the Admiral as a wall of water rushes in their direction.

Chapter 33

The spade fighter begins to hum with Sophia's touch, and the controls and instruments glow a powerful green.

"Okay, Vinny, this is going to be weird, but we are going to have to travel fast, and you'll most likely pass out, but when we get there, you'll meet the elders, and you will have to hear a bit of our history, and it might be a lot to take in so be ready," says Sophia.

Before he could respond, everything gets blurry around him, and flashes of light seem to burst off the alien canopy. A mist of water start to coat the screen as it appears that they are traveling just over the water. Soon, Vinny feels faint as his blood seems to be rushing to his feet. Everything goes black except the constant bright flashes and then no sound just darkness.

Vinny hears echoes all around him as he stands in a dark large room and feels heat from a warm bright light over his head like a spot light.

"Hello!" shouts Vinny as the echoes bounce around him.

"You, my son, you have shown the true character of mankind. What you offer to all future life is compassion, ambition, and love. The definition of life is to expand but also to learn and acquire new attributes from each new host. The focus is always to expand in technology and spirit which billions have succeeded doing before you, but none have blossomed like mankind and the focus on raw emotion defined by love. Love can be harnessed as a power to give strength and compassion to fellow man where selflessness shines among the darkest. The same love can confuse the soul and focus that untapped energy in the wrong direction blinding others of the genuine beauty it possess. Your gift is unparalled, and I ask you to search deep within your soul to save mankind from demons that coward in its presence and are humiliated by its magnificence. I offer you everlasting life of my divine love and ask that the world knows who you are. Your raw love, compassion, and ambition will shine when it's needed most. Remember, there is no alpha or omega or any false god just who was and forever will be. I am life everlasting and the creator of all you are and forever will be and grant you this gift in confidence," echoes a deep voice.

"Wake up, Vinny. We are here," says Sophia running her fingertips in his hair.

"Wow, I had the craziest dream. I was stuck in a dark hollow room confused by endless echoes. Then a light shines on me, though bright was comforting, and then it spoke telling me I'm chosen for the gift of everlasting life and to let the world know who I was," says Vinny in a relaxed tone.

"What? That just happened? There is no way you're thousands of years away," says Sophia in a concerned tone.

Vinny unmoved by the confused Sophia stares at the beautiful landscaping of the lake and surrounding mountains. Sophia rests the craft next to a flat wall on the edge of the lake and pulls a golden disc from a bag that seems to shine like the morning sun. Both Sophia and Vinny walk out of the craft and are met by locals bowing at their introduction.

"Please get up. You don't need to kneel. We only kneel to God," says Sophia in a polite tone.

Sophia walks to the flat wall with a shallow cut shaped like a door.

"You aren't going to get far," jokes Vinny.

With a smile, Sophia places the disc into an indent in the center. The ground vibrates, and the rock within the opening starts to sink within the rock exposing a brilliant light and clear bath to a world within the stone.

"Follow me, Vinny. It's time to meet the elders," asks Sophia.

As the two enter the corridor, Vinny feels weightless as they seem to float to light that gets more brilliant as they close in. The door behind gets more distant, and the hum of the local chants mellow till absolute silence. They enter the light, and a world is exposed like never seen before. A golden city with beautiful people eager to see the guests. The presence is inviting and loving as more gather, and Vinny is in awe of their appearance.

"They are beautiful, not as beautiful as you but close," giggles Vinny.

They stand tall and have flawless skin in many shades. Their hair flows like in water and shines as if it's touched by the sun. The men are lean and defined, while the woman glow in their natural beauty. Their eyes are larger but barely enough to tell and shine with every color of the rainbow.

"Tell you what, these guys would make a killing as strippers. I would pay to see them," says Vinny in a joking tone.

"Sophia, we are blessed to see you and are eager to hear your words. The council awaits, and the elders have gathered. Follow me," says one of the woman who stretches out her arm to direct them.

Standing before them is a massive structure that trivializes any church Vinny has seen before. The size is eclipsed by the brilliance of its polished gold exterior and its reflection that lights the room. Two immense doors open displaying a large room where thousands seem to be waiting. They stand in this elaborate room and soon hear a voice.

"Welcome, Sophia. You were missed. To our guest, welcome. We are the Annunaki."

Chapter 34

The wall of water rushes toward the Atlantic fleet and appears to have a menacing grin the closer it gets. The eager displaced water seems intent on unleashing some fury on the idle fleet.

"We are going to feel this one, my friends," shouts Admiral Gray.

The wall of water collides with the anticipating fleet with explicit force stirring the ships like a toddler playing with bath toys. There shimmers an odd blue glow as the heated ocean turned to plasma from the impact of the space rod. In the distance, you hear the vicious roar of the passing wave, and in the bridge, you hear the sighs of relief.

"Well holy shit that was a big wave. What's the damage around the fleet?" asks the admiral.

"All clear, sir, a couple of the smaller ships are reporting some heavy flooding in the engine rooms but have begun to pump most of it out. It would appear the Russian fleet is in complete disarray," says a bridge officer.

In the distance, you see black smoke as it darkens the sky from the heavily damaged fleet. The Russian aircraft carrier is almost resting on its side, and the hole from the rail gun has exposed the inside of the ship almost splitting it in two. The radar shows at least two subs that remain stationary and are marked within about a thousand yards of the rods impact. This battle has shown the once weakened United States military is back with a serious sign of strength. The space rod and rail gun are game changers, and the world was not ready. The president has shown the world that America is back and on the path of recovery and even in the darkest hour will remain diligent in its beliefs and freedoms.

"Let's not get too worked up yet. Thirty minutes ago, we had a trick up our sleeve, and we had a combined fleet of both Russians, Iranians, and alien headed toward us hell-bent on kicking our ass. The big question was why did the alien crafts break and leave the others high and dry? Did they detect the space rods or rail gun knowing the destructive forces they possess? Something isn't right, and until we have serious answers, we need to assume this is just the beginning," says the admiral.

In the distance, the black smoke separates as alien craft begins to break through. The large vessel hovers a few hundred feet above the sinking aircraft carrier, while hundreds of the spade fighters seem to surround it like a swarm of killer bees. A glowing beam seems to project from the large vessel and engulfs the bridge of the dying ship. Within the beam, you see something being extracted from the ship as it's pulled on board.

"This is far from over," says the admiral as he calls for battle stations.

Blood soaks the tattered uniform, and pain overwhelms Admiral Ivanov as he lays on a cold floor. He looks up as blood trickles into his eyes blurring his vision of the beings surrounding him. Admiral Ivanov coughs deep from within his chest, and a brilliant taste of iron fills his mouth as blood fills his hand.

"You are dying, Admiral," says a voice in the distance.

"This is the end of a life you thought you knew, but I alone can save you from death. I alone can give you life eternal, but I ask you to do one thing," says a voice.

The voice inches closer, and soon, shimmers of light reveal Amun who lowers himself to the dying admiral's level.

"Your people will die. The Americans have shown a force your government was not prepared for. You need to act now to save your people. Below us are two nuclear submarines and with your codes you can send over two hundred nuclear warheads to all that oppose us. You also command the codes to release the nuclear torpedoes that will create a contaminated tsunami of radioactive water five hundred feet high. If you act now, the world will fall and kneel to the Asuras, and you will be divine and the savior of your people, and they will inherit this new earth. We have your computers synced, and all it needs is your code, and the world is yours," says Amun.

The admiral desperate for life and the pride of his nation enters the codes.

Within moments, a rumbling can be felt throughout the ship's hulls, and hundreds of blasts are seen coming from the ocean surface. The sky becomes littered with hundreds of blood-thirsty ICBMs destined for cities all over the world.

"Oh my god, there are hundreds of them. These nuclear missiles will wipe out everyone never mind the fall out. I have to contact the president and make them aware and prepare them for Armageddon," shouts Admiral Gray. "Get all the jets we can in the air, and intercept as many of the warheads as possible. Use the Ghost Squad too. Do all we can to take as many of these things down," Admiral Gray continues.

"Sir, it's Washington. They see the warheads on radar and have started evacuation processes, but the president wants to speak to you direct," says an ensign.

"Hey, Terence, I am sorry I failed," says Admiral Gray in a defeated tone

"Listen, open a file I just sent you. There are some more tricks up our sleeve. It won't be all, but most of the missiles can be taken care of with operation Killer Swarm. This will unleash thousands of mini drones from warheads on the Lexington II. They will explode at around sixty thousand feet, and the drones all contain military-grade explosives. The drones will systematically attach themselves to each ICBM and detonate destroying the warheads. We are launching five more space rods on military targets, but you need to launch those rockets now and get the drones flying," orders the president.

"Yes, sir. They are launching in less than ten seconds," shouts the admiral.

Hatches explode, and splashes are heard as the modified rockets scream toward the stratosphere. From the overcast skies melded with black smoke of the dying Russian fleet, you hear an eerie thunderous crack and an ominous glow of blue break from the atmosphere. The space rods break through the clouds and head toward its target and before the image can be absorbed; a magnificent flash is seen in the far distance followed by noxious roar as the first rod meets the target.

"My god, this is the end of life as we know it, and the aliens got what they wanted," says Admiral Gray as a flash is seen when his rockets explode releasing thousands of drones.

"Great day to die huh, Captain?" asks the admiral.

"Sir, yes, sir, great day to die a beautiful death."

Chapter 35

Vinny stands in awe of this astonishing room and the brilliance of the features inside it. The ceilings are grand, and in each corner of the room stand golden statues of cloaked beings with their hands held out. The room holds hundreds of elegant beings laced in shinning silky garb. The image is of ancient gothic architecture that invites the soul and accents the brilliance of the people who dwell within.

"Thank you for the warm welcome, and I am sorry I keep staring, but this is a lot to take in," says Vinny.

"Sophia, why have you brought him to a sacred place and exposed the Annunaki? We cannot interfere with the progress of man unless they violate the laws set by the gift givers of life before us," says a deep tone from a lifted stage in front of them.

"I understand, father, but the Asuras have exposed themselves. They have demanded allegiance and labeled themselves divine. They have declared that they are the rightful gift givers and that mankind will be judged and that a purge is inevitable. They have identified a merging gene that allows the human body to meld with the Asura's DNA creating hybrids. They have hybrid clone toddlers in the ocean below that seems to carry the same destructive trait of essence displacement until they found Ethan. Ethan did not reject the Asura's DNA, and by doing so, they can map a specific gene structure. Father, they have found their Adam," says Sophia.

"This is impossible. We made sure that they couldn't splice their genes into any other life-form," says the voice.

"Father, this was Vinny's best friend. I knew he was dying, and as I brushed his face to help him find comfort, I knew not even my essence could help him. As soon as I saw the Asuras and the world they created under the sea, I knew we underestimated them. Then a rejuvenated Ethan walks in the room, and he was healed of all his wounds, but when I touched him, I knew this wasn't the same being I met. His essence was dark and his character was missing, and then he showed a mark on his right hand, a bio tracker that identified his DNA pattern. Amun still sits on his throne, and he said that the Asuras will judge, and only specific DNA signatures would result in the honor of the mark, and I feel it's just those they discovered can merge with Asura's DNA. The part that was most disturbing is that they wanted Vinny, a man I have grown to love," says Sophia as she grabs Vinny's hand. "Vinny, this is my father Enki."

The introduction was quick as members of a council seem to converge on Enki. Soon, Enki steps aside and walks toward Vinny. Enki is in every way impressive and showed such an amazing presence that Vinny felt emotional.

"We are the Annunaki the keepers of life. We have been given the honor of assisting in the path of new life and to find the next keepers of life. We are given specific rules on the stages of this transformation bestowed on mankind and by no accounts allowed to deviate from the written path. Your world is in chaos, and we weep as the carnage continues to ravage the innocent. We weep as children are murdered and raped by the greed of man. We weep as nation after nation wage war in the name of adolescent differences masked by false gods. We weep as the beauty of mankind is stained by the ego of one's color, heritage, or preference of who they love. Murderers, thieves, and villains rule your kind fueled by greed and power, and we weep asking what we have created. The world continues to die, and we never have intervened because it's up to humanity to discover resolve. If your world dies, you die with it, but if you survive the chaos, then you evolve to higher level of being. You see life's magnificence and shed your hate and restricting ego. You learn to become one being and not separate nationalities or races. Your learn love and to love and that it has no bounds and cannot be judged by close-minded hypocrite's force-feeding opinions. You do this not because we taught you it but because you experienced defeat and loss and from those ashes of torment you rise up. This is the path of experiencing life, and all previous beings and gift keepers learned to fail before understanding and appreciating success. Who are we to change the right to fail, holding back the opportunity to succeed? We would be teaching you that failure is a flaw and that someone or something will always pick you up and that there are no repercussions for your damaged ego and desperate hate. We will not lead you into temptation and resolve only to see you stay the same. You either survive or die knowing that you failed to see a gift, the everlasting gift of life and peace, divine love, and respect for all living things and appreciation for being more than a smart ape. I am sorry you wasted your time coming here looking for our salvation, but we offer you comfort in that life will always continue," says Enki.

Vinny stares at Enki with a sense of intimidation combined with reverence but realizes Enki seems to be judging mankind the same way the Asuras did. There isn't time to choose words, but Vinny feels compelled to say how he feels.

"I understand there are rules and strict guidelines for something as important as life. I can comfortably say life has new meaning for me after the past few days, learning to believe in God not religion and seeing love in the purest form for Sophia and loss of my friend. I also weep as I see the world that I contribute to slowly die, and at times, I feel lacks resolve. I heard a hundred stories of people rising up from the ashes to be better only to be balanced by other stories where people use despair as an excuse for failure. My issue is that your explanation lacks validity, and it is flawed. Never has there been a second gift giver destined to see a species fail, correct? If we are meant to fail by our own hands and rise from ashes, how does the influence of a rogue race play into your rules, a race you developed? To add depth to your lack of detail, isn't what the Asuras are doing a mirror image of your protocol? They have failed, and in the chaos, they rose up to survive, and you challenged them by telling them they are not worthy even though they see themselves as existing on a higher plain. Wouldn't any species oppressed stand up to the boot that is pressed on their head? What I hear is that unless we are just like you, then we are not worthy of your gift and what rises from the ashes better mirror you or you will proceed to turn your back on anything not like you and assist in their extinction. You Enki are a hypocrite blinded by your own perspective, and you are right in that. I'm sorry I wasted my time coming here!" says Vinny in a stern tone.

"The Asuras and their science was an abomination and an absolute insult to the gift of life and blessing of essence!" shouts back Enki.

"Their ideas and defiance of the rules of the gift of life could not be tolerated. They used science to extract essence and that defiance began to kill them and as they died so did millions of years of progress. They would have tainted the core of life, and any generation after them would have used essence on a scientific and physical form not spiritual. Amun and his son are all that remain of a dead world, and they cannot procreate, so they are doomed to not exist. They have created hybrids and unnatural creatures to extend their inevitable demise. They have no spirit, and the ashes they rose from are the same ashes they brought here to smother you. The rules don't state what the chaos has to be, a villainous race, a killer asteroid, or an incurable disease. Chaos is chaos, and you will have to rise up or drown in the same ashes they bestowed upon you."

"With all due respect, you're a coward. This abomination is your creation and our failure will rest at your feet as your failure. The end results will be genocide, and mankind will be depleted. They have sworn to inherit this planet by merging with my species, and then you will have a new war as two species combined into one rise from the ashes dedicated to your annihilation. I expected more. As I passed out coming here, a brilliant light, pure light, that warmed my soul spoke to my very being. What was said engulfed my soul, and each word resonates inside me."

"My son, you have shown true character of mankind. What you offer to all life is compassion, ambition, and love. The definition of life is not just to expand but to learn and acquire new attributes from each new host. None have blossomed like mankind with your focus of raw emotion defined by love. Your gift is unparalleled Vinny; I need you to search your soul to save mankind. The demons coward in the emotion of loves divine presence and they are intimidated by its magnificence. I offer you everlasting life of my divine love and ask the world to know who you are. I am everlasting and the creator of all you are and forever will be and grant you this gift in confidence" (the room gasps).

"Mankind has no need for your conceded point of view, and we sure don't need two aliens judging us eager to enforce our failure. I now feel the need to lead mankind to rise up and defend ourselves against those that oppose us, to unite mankind in love and understanding or die for the very love I now believe in. I am sorry, Sophia."

The room stares in confusion, and several other Annunaki surround Enki and Sophia. Sophia walks quickly to meet up with Vinny to let him know the concern.

"Okay, Vinny, the council needs to convene because two things just happened. One it would appear a massive battle has begun, and over two hundred nuclear warheads have been fired by the Russians threating all life not just mankind. Two which is crazy is you have been blessed by Elohim and given a divine gift of everlasting life. You have been chosen by Elohim to be awarded the next level. This has never been recorded this early. This gift is usually presented to a spiritual being at the highest level. No Asuras has been ever awarded this vision and promise, and it's why my father knew they are not a chosen race. The Asuras are prepared to deploy reapers and challenge this earth to extinction, and their hybrids will inherit it. My father is the only Annunaki to receive the same gift you received, and he was the savior of our species. We now believe you to be the savior of mankind and the one to help them rise from the ashes. The elders will support you, and this now begins a new holy war for the very survival of the gift of life. By receiving this gift, you and I can now be together, live out our remaining days together. I love you, Vinny, and this battle will be hard, and the loss of all life will be catastrophic, but we will rise up together and unify mankind, and the gift of life will radiate in all you are and all of mankind."

Vinny walks out the large doors with Sophia, and Annunaki whisper and bow their heads to show respect. They are led to another large opening and before them are thousands of ships reflecting like gold shields. In the room, a vibration is felt, and soon, the sun kisses the grand corridor, and the shimmer of brilliance reflects off the craft and on to Vinny's face. As Vinny takes in the room, he feels a hand touch his shoulder. He looks and sees a strong defined hand, and his eyes walk up the arm and shoulder and sees the face of Enki.

"There was something about your spirit that mesmerized me, Vinny. There was something special in my daughter's eyes when she looked at you that our people have not been exposed to. The elders and I agree that mankind is worth fighting for, but I believe you're worth dying for. My forces are deploying now to balance out the power, and in a moment, I will have you contact your president so he knows that he has support, and we can discuss the battle ahead," says Enki with a comforting grin.

"Thank you, but getting my president on the phone, I mean, I don't even have his number. What about the nuclear warheads spread out all over the globe?" asks Vinny.

A whistle is heard, and soon, he sees hundreds or perhaps thousands of the golden shields racing across the sky at insane speeds. Enki looks at Vinny with a slight chuckle and says, "Let me know when you're ready, and we will tap you right into the president."

Brilliant light pops before each vessel as if teleporting to another place, while Vinny seems eager to see how he will talk to the president. A slight hum is heard, and the hairs on Vinny's arms stand up as a purple and black hole seems to rip into the air in front of him. Sophia feeling his concern grabs his hand to comfort him, and Enki grips the back of his neck in comfort giving small taps. Sophia leads Vinny into the darken space, and Vinny feels the weight of Enki behind him. Vinny looks at his hands, and they seem to shake violently causing them to blur, and the space he is in seems to stretch giving depth to a void. The hum now resonates in Vinny's head, and his stomach feels like it did when his mom went over small hills in cars. Vinny feels the throw up nearing the back of his teeth, but in that moment, a flash of light startles him, and as he opens his eyes, he is standing before the president and several armed men.

"Give me a second. I can't get use to this shit," says Vinny as he holds back vomiting at the president's feet.

"Put the guns down. Our prays are answered," says the president.

Enki stands there with an almost divine presence, and he allows a second for everyone to grasp what just happened.

"Vinny, Sophia, who is this?" asks the president.

"This is my father Enki, and Vinny convinced them to help mankind but under one request," says Sophia. "This assistance is meant for all humanity not just America and its allies. This marks the beginning of a new world and a war for its very survival, and though we all know who the leaders are, Vinny is mankind's savior."

"What does that mean?" asks the president.

"It means Elohim has given him the gift of everlasting life. He will bring together mankind and help shed their battered ego and get them to focus on tranquility. You are about to see death at a level that you cannot recover from, and we are here to stop it. We are the Annunaki, the watchers from the heavens in which we came. We are here to teach the gift of life and to graduate mankind to the next level. Elohim has spoken to Vinny, and he will unite us all, but first, we need to stop the carnage," says Enki.

Before the president can respond, an intern rushes out and says, "They are exploding everywhere. The grid is collapsing, and thousands of golden crafts all over the world are battling the spade fighters and destroying the nukes."

The president with secret service and national guard troops in tow rush out to the city landscape. Brilliant flashes of light expose the golden craft as they seem to appear in the thousands. Each craft rapidly fires red bursts of energy at the Asura's craft that seems to shred the protective shield. The sky becomes alive with swarms of battling alien craft. The president mesmerized by the violent chaos sees an intimidating tall man stand next to him. Enki with a grin looks up at the sky as ships three-city blocks in size flash and then hover over the Hudson River and says, "This war will be the death of all that was and the Asuras and breathe new life into a new world. This war ends all wars, and this end will give birth to a new world."

Chapter 36

The haze is thick of death and destruction, and as the admiral looks up at the poisoned sky, it is stained by a swarm of alien craft and drones. The image sinks the admiral's stomach as a crack of a second rod echoes in the distance.

"Sir, we have something odd on the radar," says the operator.

"What is it now?" asks the admiral.

"Blips keep flashing on the screen in the thousands, some large some small. The images are literally appearing out of thin air, and they seem to be engaging the grid!" says the operator.

"Get the president on the phone!" says the admiral, but before he can connect, the phone rings.

"Hold on to your ass, Daniel. Shit is going to be crazy. We got our own aliens! Do not engage on any of the gold discs. They are allies and will subdue the Asuras and neutralize all the nukes. I have cancelled the remaining rods, and I have some new advisors headed your way and will be on your forward deck in a moment," says the president in a renewed tone.

"I see a distortion on the deck. What the hell is this shit, Terence? It is spinning and turning purple and black," replies the admiral.

"It's Enki, the Annunaki leader which is the race flying those gold discs. He will work directly with you to battle the Asuras. He will arrive with his daughter Sophia and Vinny who has been declared the savior of mankind, be Elohim," replies the president.

"Have you lost your goddamn mind? What the hell is an Enki and Elohim? Not to mention Sophia and a savior Vinny, where the hell are they from, Saturn?" says the admiral in a concerned tone.

"No, the Bronx," replies the president.

On the deck, the distorted opening exposes Enki, Sophia, and Vinny as they head toward the bridge. Flash after flash appears above the Lexington II as gold discs converge to start forming a protective barrier.

"They dare to defy me!" shouts Amun. "They have gained support of the Annunaki, and they attack us!"

"The discs have destroyed all the nuclear warheads and now attack the fighters holding the grid," says Yhovah.

"It's time to unleash hell and rid the Annunaki of all future life. They cannot be allowed to rule over mankind and take their conceded interpretation of the gift any further. They judged us and killed all the Asuras and our world. We are all that is left, but the prophecy says we will rise up from that chaos to graduate to the next level. Deploy all our ships and release all the reapers now. I want to focus all the firepower on that lead ship. This war ends and will have our rightful place as the superior race and the future keepers of life and the future watchers of our hybrid race destined for greatness," says Amun with a clenched fist.

The ocean becomes alive again, and the grid begins to fall from the previous discipline. Rising from the ocean, large craft head in several directions destined to drop their payload of death harnessed by the reapers. Amun waves his hand over the controls and presses his hand on a clear screen that soon activates the reapers. Within moments, the cells holding the reapers show sign of life, and as they wake, the sound of their screams sends chills over the Asuras monitoring them. Their mouths appear sealed, and as they scream, flesh stretches across their narrow openings. Their eyes are pearl white water with hatred and lack any hint of a soul. They each hold a rod, and at the end is a blade like a scythe. A tube runs from the shaft to a large pack on their back, and a heinous hum blends with their screams.

"Be sure to deploy them in the cities first. The flies in their packs are capable of infecting over two million per each reaper clan, but it can hurt us too," says Amun.

"Father, they are within minutes of reaching over two hundred location," says Yhovah.

"Unleash the devils and watch as hell takes over this earth," shouts Amun as the flaps behind his head rise up.

As the craft reach the cities, the containers open exposing the wicked reapers as they thrash around merged with their eerie screams. The golden discs begin firing at the crafts while defending themselves from the now menacing grid that has divided and challenges them. As the craft get low, a swarm of reapers fall out from the belly of the craft and blanket the cities. The moment they land, they begin waving their scythe around unleashing millions of poisoned flies into the air, and any unfortunate person nearby is ripped apart by the blades.

"The purge has begun. Now to take care of the Annunaki," says Amun.

He grips the controls of the craft and screams as thousands of pins penetrate his arms and hands tapping into his ancient essence. The craft glows in a deep purple and soon appears almost black. Amun continues to screams as the essence drains from his being, and as the flesh-like horns rise up, again he screams as a blast of energy black as night fires at the Lexington II.

Enki turns and sees as the pure evil essence impacts the bow of the ship thrusting him several yards through the air. The golden shields shift position to evade a second shot. Enki, slightly dazed, looks and sees the impact was devastating exposing the second deck of the venerable ship. Then a noise rips apart his ears and enters his soul. He quickly turns and sees Vinny screaming and holding a lifeless Sophia in his arms. Enki rushes over and sees the tattered blood-soaked body of his daughter and the raw emotion in Vinny's scream. Enki drops to his knees and in agony weeps in torment. He rests his hand on the leg of his beautiful child brushing away her blood-soaked hair to expose the peace in her face. He turns to Vinny and rests his hand on his shoulder trying to comfort the pain evident in the cries bellowing from Vinny's soul. Enki gathers himself as warmth surrounds him and is taken back as the veins in Vinny's hands and arms glow brilliant red.

"They will pay for this, and they will suffer for what they did to Sophia," shouts Vinny as the red glow seems to accent every vein in his body. Vinny softly rests Sophia on the deck, stands up, and boldly says, "This is not over."

About the Author

Michael Piccirilli was born and raised just outside New York City in the city of Peekskill. Michael grew up in a single-parent home with his role model being his amazing mother. Early in his childhood, Michael was exposed to a strict religious upbringing due to his mother being a member of a born-again Christian church. In that church, Michael was hounded and haunted with the consequences of sin but questioned much of what was taught. Soon after graduating, Michael joined the US Navy and finished serving in the US Coast Guard spending time around the ocean. Michael now resides an hour outside of Boston in Southern Seacoast of New Hampshire. In the past several years, Michael has researched the ancient alien theory and was fascinated by the similarities between the Bible, religion, and a possible alien influenced past. Michael besides writing enjoys watching his daughters play softball and spending time with his family Tania, Sophia, and Aaliyah.

CPSIA information can be obtained
at www.ICGtesting.com
Printed in the USA
BVHW081236061221
623331BV00007B/198